CREATIVE WOMAN MYSTERIES®

Deadliest in Show

# Christy Barritt

Annie's®

AnniesFiction.com

Library of Congress-in-Publication Data
Deadliest in Show / by Christy Barritt
p. cm.
I. Title
                            2013940217

AnniesFiction.com
800-282-6643
Creative Woman Mysteries
Series Editor: Shari Lohner

10 11 12 13 14 | Printed in China | 9 8 7 6 5 4 3

# — 1 —

"**I** would kill to have talent like yours!"

Shannon McClain smiled at the group of women who gathered around the displays at her table, admiring her handcrafted jewelry. They'd been at her booth at the art-and-craft show for the past twenty-five minutes, going back and forth on which necklace and bracelet they each should purchase. For a moment—just a moment—Shannon felt like a celebrity as they gushed over her work.

She came back down to earth long enough to give a reasonable response to their sweet comments. "Well, it's part talent and part hard work, but thank you. I'll take the compliments." Her Scottish accent lilted with each word.

Shannon had to admit that she loved hearing the fuss over her creations. She'd worked hard to develop her jewelry, and it was nice to see the payoff. Since she sold much of her jewelry online, she didn't always get to see her customers' faces light up with admiration.

She'd spent the past several weeks designing elegant jewelry to sell at the first ever West Coast Art and Fine Craft Festival. Everyone in Apple Grove had been delighted when their city had been chosen out of several in Washington and Oregon to host the prestigious show, organized by the Artists Guild of the Northwest.

A three-day event, it was taking place in the local high

school gym, which was packed with exhibitors who displayed only high-quality work. But the gym was also packed with customers hoping to get an early start on their Christmas shopping—or at least that's what several people had told Shannon.

There was so much competition to get into the show. Only the best of the best had been chosen by the jury over-seeing the application process. Shannon could see why. The Guild had done a great job of advertising, and people from up and down the coast had traveled to attend the event.

The three women at her booth, who said they'd driven down from Portland, finally picked the items they wanted and paid. They walked away happy customers, which made Shannon one happy jewelry maker.

"You've had no shortage of compliments over your work." The voice beside Shannon startled her.

Sunny Davis, whose adjacent booth featured her stained glass art, had slipped up beside Shannon as she served cus-tomers. Shannon and Sunny had chatted quite a bit on Thursday in between customers, and Shannon felt like the two were kindred spirits.

"I certainly can't complain. Nor can you, apparently." Shannon nodded toward Sunny's booth, where half of her beautiful masterpieces had already been purchased. "It looks like you're going to sell out."

Sunny glanced down at her table. "I like doing shows like these. They remind me of my roots. This is where it all started for me."

Shannon pointed to the magazine article displayed on Sunny's table. *The Artist's Touch* was one of the top arts-and-crafts magazines in the country, and the cover featured Sunny. "It certainly doesn't appear that someone of your caliber would need to do a craft show to promote your work."

Sunny sipped from her bottle of flavored water. "You do some things out of logic. Other things you do from your heart. These shows help feed my heart, if you know what I mean."

"I understand. My friends convinced me to apply for the show. When I was accepted, I decided I'd donate my profits to a local charity. It seemed like a win-win situation that way." Shannon's friends in the Purls of Hope knitting club had also agreed to help her out during the show so she wouldn't have to man her booth alone.

Sunny's eyes lit up. "What a great idea! I'll have to do that the next time someone asks me to enter a show." Her hands went to her hips. "Better yet, maybe we could plan a whole show where *all* profits go to a charity. Wouldn't that be fun?"

Shannon had to agree. "That sounds like a fabulous idea."

"Let's exchange cards and talk about it sometime after this weekend."

"It's a deal."

A group of women meandering to her booth pulled Sunny away from the friendly exchange, and Shannon turned away just in time to see a familiar figure approach her table.

"If it isn't Shannon McClain."

A casual grin on his face, Michael Stone stopped at her table and fingered a leaf-print necklace. He watched her, the detective in him easily trumping his friendly demeanor. He was always observing, always taking mental notes of everything around him. In his forties, with close-cropped black hair, blue eyes, and a six-foot-plus height, Michael had the rugged good looks of a TV detective—but he was the real deal. He co-owned the private investigation and security consulting firm Stone & McCrary.

Shannon scolded her heart for skipping a couple of beats when their eyes met. She'd accepted the fact that he was romantically off limits. He still had ghosts from his past to make peace with before he'd be ready for another relationship. In her mind, she *knew* this. So why did she react this way whenever she saw the man?

She cleared her throat. "Michael. What a pleasure. I didn't see you as an art show kind of guy."

He shrugged, his overcoat damp from the drizzle outside. "I was out and about, and decided to see what everyone's making such a big fuss over. This show is all I keep hearing about around town."

She spread her arms out like a game show hostess, as if displaying the entire showcase floor "Well, things are sure hopping. There is indeed reason for all the fuss."

Shannon's gaze traveled upward until it met Michael's again. His piercing blue eyes were perceptive and breathtakingly beautiful. But they weren't hers to stare at. They were just friends, and it was better that way. "So what really brings you out this way?" she asked.

"I'm on my way home from a job. I just happened to be passing by." His eyes twinkled. "I thought I'd stop and say hello."

"Well, I appreciate the gesture. Have you walked around yet?" She nodded toward the rest of the showroom floor, where forty of the region's best had their works displayed.

"I saw you when I walked in and came right over. Your booth is hard to miss, and I didn't give the others much more than a glance."

"You're right. I couldn't have asked for better placement." Truly, she'd gotten a great spot, not very far from the entrance where almost all the show's guests were certain to walk past. "Would you care to stroll around a bit?"

He smiled. "With you? Yes, I'd love to."

Shannon saw her friend Joyce Buchanan walking toward her with a steaming cup of coffee in hand and waved. Joyce's wide grin nearly matched the sparkling beads on her shirt. Bedazzling was her favorite thing to do, and not one clothing item or accessory seemed to go untouched. A member of the Purls of Hope, Joyce was in her mid-forties; she had platinum blond hair and a full figure. She was also a member of the local artists guild. Though Joyce was volunteering for the entire show, Shannon felt fortunate to get most of her attention. Shannon knew that Joyce didn't take time away from her bakery, Pink Sprinkles, very often, but she'd lined up assistants at the shop to help out during the art show this weekend.

"Am I ever glad to see you."

"Who isn't?" Joyce asked with a grin and an exaggerated poof of her hair.

"Precisely. But I do have ulterior motives. Do you think you could watch my booth for a moment? I'd like to stretch my legs a bit."

Joyce winked. "Sure thing."

Shannon joined Michael on the glossy wooden floor of the gym. They stopped almost immediately to admire Sunny's work. She had made gorgeous light catchers to hang in windows, as well as lampshades and night-lights. Sunny was helping a customer, so Shannon simply waved.

"I'll introduce you to Sunny later. She's the sweetest lady," Shannon told Michael. "We're lucky to have such a high-profile artist at the show."

Michael peered closer at one of the items on the table. "One of those lamps might look good in my office. What do you think?"

Shannon felt flattered he'd asked her opinion. Usually he avoided anything that hinted that their relationship might be anything but professional. They had had only one date, and that had almost ended in disaster. Since then, their interactions had been, at best, awkward. "I think you're right," she agreed. "That would look lovely."

"Hey, Shannon." Sunny stepped closer as her customer left. "Stretching your legs for a bit?"

"I have trouble sitting still for too long."

Sunny grinned. "I understand that." She extended her hand toward Michael. "Sunny Davis."

"Michael Stone. Nice to meet you. Your work is beautiful."

"Thanks." She rubbed her temples. "I'm hoping I'll be able to make the entire show this weekend."

"Is something wrong?" Shannon asked.

She shook her head. "Just a headache. Maybe a bug. It seems to happen every year at this time—with the seasons changing and all. Perhaps I need to start taking vitamins to boost my immune system."

Shannon nodded. "Drink lots of orange juice too."

As another customer approached, Shannon and Michael excused themselves and continued their walk around the gym.

"So, the show is going well?" Michael asked as they jostled through the crowds.

"There are some great artists here—some of the best on the West Coast, if not in the nation. The level of craftsmanship is outstanding. I'm honored to be a part of it."

"I'm just glad that you're doing this instead of being caught up in solving some crime." He offered a wry smile.

Shannon couldn't resist a playful elbow to his side. "You do realize that I don't *look* for mysteries to solve—right? They seem to find me."

He frowned. "That's what worries me."

"I worry you?" She watched his expression with a strange sense of amusement.

"I don't want to see you get hurt."

The sincerity in his eyes caused her heart to do an inadvertent flip.

She cleared her throat. "I appreciate that."

A short, balding man stopped in front of them. He had his smartphone in hand and an air of briskness about him. "Are you Shannon McClain?"

"I am." Shannon didn't recognize the man, so she regarded him cautiously.

He extended his free hand. "I'm Rupert Murphy, and I'm the president of R & M Designs. I've been keeping an eye on your work for awhile now."

R & M Designs was one of the premier jewelry companies in the country. Their unique pieces were found in jewelry stores in malls from the Pacific to the Atlantic. Shannon grasped his hand, and he pumped it briefly. "I'm honored that you've even heard of me," she said.

He glanced at his phone before sliding it into his pocket and putting his hands on his hips. "I've been studying your designs, and your work is really outstanding. Your pieces have a unique touch that sets them apart from others."

"Thank you. I appreciate that." Pride surged in her. She'd put a lot of work into her jewelry, and it was lovely to be noticed.

"I'd like to talk to you sometime when you have a free minute and things aren't so hectic."

"If you don't mind me asking—about what?" She couldn't even begin to fathom where he might be going with this. Perhaps it had something to do with her business, the Paisley Craft Market & Artist Lofts.

The man's lip curled into a half smile. "About coming to work for me."

"Coming to work for *you*?" Shannon's heart stuttered a beat, noticeably enough that she raised her hand to cover her chest. "Wow. I'm flattered."

He handed her a business card and an envelope and then peered at her through his bushy eyebrows. "Call me. I can make you a really nice offer that would get you out of this little rinky-dink town. We can have your work in all of my stores nationwide. I can make you a household name."

Shannon opened her mouth, ready to defend Apple Grove, but before she could respond, Rupert slipped back into the crowd. She stared at his card a moment before stuffing it into the back pocket of her jeans. When she looked up, she saw Michael studying her.

"Sounds like you're about to hit it big time. Even *I've* heard of R & M Designs, and I'm by no means a jewelry guy." Admiration shone in his gaze.

She blinked, still in shock over the brief conversation.

"I don't know. That was so unexpected. I don't even know what to think."

"Sounds like a once-in-a-lifetime opportunity. You should call him. It's about time someone recognized your talent. You do a lot for other people. You should consider doing something for yourself."

"But he mentioned something about leaving Apple Grove. Why would I want to do that? I love it here ..." She shook her head and began walking again. "I've got to let that sink in some more. Besides, I don't want to jump to conclusions. I haven't even heard everything he has to say yet."

As they walked past a table displaying homemade candles, the fragrances of cinnamon and lilacs wafted up. Scents were in abundance at the show, from candles and handcrafted soaps and lotions to the food court catered by a local restaurant in town that was known for its soups.

Shannon's stomach rumbled at the thought of food. Lunch remained a couple of hours away, and she regretted her meager breakfast now. She should have packed some apple slices or a granola bar.

Pausing in front of a woodcarver's booth—a man who did beautiful scroll-saw work on a variety of items including room dividers, wall hangings, and Christmas ornaments—Shannon couldn't help but overhear the conversation between him and the show organizer, Mark Arnold. Shannon had heard Mark was a real stickler for details. In her brief interactions with him, Mark's prickly ways hinted at a perfectionist personality. That could work well for running a business, but not so well for interpersonal relationships.

Michael leaned closer. "That looks like a heated exchange."

Shannon nodded, uncomfortable that the two men were arguing in public. "Not sure that will serve as the best publicity for the show. You can teach a lot of things, but you can't teach people skills."

"I can't argue with that."

"Shannon!"

Shannon turned her head toward the sound. *Who now?* These shows were like reunions for all the artsy residents in the community, including the people who often shopped in Shannon's store.

She looked around and spotted Hunter Banks standing a short distance away, looking a little damp from the rainy weather. Hunter, a biologist with Bayside Marine Research Associates, had come to town a couple of months earlier. He was tall, with sandy hair, deeply tanned skin, and green eyes that sparkled with life. His gaze left hers and locked with Michael's.

Tension stretched between the two men like wire between two highline poles.

*It must be my imagination*, she thought. It had to be. Michael hadn't expressed any intentions toward her besides friendship for a while now. And although the attention from Hunter felt flattering, she wasn't a schoolgirl prone to crushes. She considered herself a professional woman who remained in total control of her emotions.

Most of the time.

She cleared her throat. "Good to see you, Hunter. What an unexpected surprise."

He returned his focus to Shannon and grinned. "I didn't want to miss the opportunity to see my favorite girl."

Shannon nodded toward the aisle in front of them. "We were just walking around and enjoying some of the work here. Would you care to join us?"

"I'd love to."

As the three began to walk, with Shannon sandwiched in the middle, she couldn't ignore the awkwardness of the situation. What exactly could she talk about with these two men simultaneously, other than the weather or football? Her idea of football was what they would call soccer, and neither had admitted to being a soccer fan. So the conversation seemed destined to be about the dreary weather. After they'd discussed it at length, they all fell silent.

Michael cleared his throat before nodding toward the food court. "How about I go get us some coffee?"

"Sounds good," Shannon said. "Could you check and see if they have tea? Earl Grey?"

He smiled. "Of course." His grin slipped as he turned toward Hunter. "And you? Would you care for anything?"

Hunter shook his head, droplets of water from the rain outside dripping onto his jacket as his eyes danced with … was it amusement? "I'm good. Drank a Thermos of coffee on my way here."

Michael mumbled something and slipped away, leaving Hunter and Shannon to peruse the aisles of handcrafts alone. Hunter picked up a hand-painted ostrich egg. "Impressive."

"And expensive." She pointed to the price tag. "Be careful with that."

His eyebrows shot up, and he set it back down carefully. "Noted. I had no idea eggs were so expensive."

They braved the jostling crowds again, pausing to note

various pieces of art. Finally, Hunter turned toward her and spoke. "So, I have an ulterior motive for stopping by today."

"Do you?"

"Yes. I hoped maybe we could go to dinner sometime this week." He paused. "What do you think?"

Shannon was so accustomed to Michael keeping his distance that hearing someone actually be forward about his intentions threw her off kilter. Despite that, her first instinct was to say no. However, her friends in the Purls had scolded her often of late about not giving anyone a chance. Perhaps it was time to push herself outside her comfort zone.

She smiled, though it felt forced. "I'd love to. Why don't you give me a call when I have my calendar nearby, and we'll confirm a time and date?"

"That sounds perfect." He glanced at his watch. "Look, I've gotta run. I just wanted to catch you here and see your beautiful face for a moment."

He was quite the charmer, Shannon had to admit. His attention was sweet and flattering, and it added a dose of excitement to her life.

In a great twist of timing, Hunter slipped away just as Michael appeared with her steaming cup of tea.

"He sure left quickly." Michael watched him leave and took a sip of his hot coffee. Black, Shannon had no doubt. He was a no-frills kind of guy.

She shrugged. "I guess he didn't have much time."

"Interesting." Michael turned toward her. "I hate to abandon you also, but I need to get going. Maybe we'll catch up over coffee and tea another time?"

Shannon smiled. "I'd like that." She raised her cup. "And thanks for the drink."

"Anytime, Shannon."

She was still smiling when she returned to her booth.

Joyce raised her eyebrows, her gaze following Michael in the distance. Shannon had no doubt her friend had seen the whole exchange.

"I do believe that you have two men vying for your attention," Joyce said.

Shannon flicked her hand in the air, setting her sterling silver bracelets jangling. "Nonsense. They're both just friends."

Joyce chuckled, shaking her head. "Men like Michael and Hunter do not stop by craft shows just for the fun of it." She pulled out a powder compact and a tube of lipstick and began to reapply her trademark fuchsia color to her lips. "You're beautiful and smart and creative, and those men have obviously noticed that."

Shannon started to speak, but stopped. She had no idea how to argue with a compliment like that, so she decided that she wouldn't. "Let's just concentrate on the show. It's like the Super Bowl of crafters. Let's not waste our time talking about men."

"Two handsome men, I should add." Joyce wagged her eyebrows and grinned.

Shannon laughed at her friend's silly antics before letting her gaze peruse the showroom floor again. There appeared to be a lot of happy customers wandering about, talking to the exhibitors.

Her gaze stopped at her neighbor. She squinted when she saw Sunny. The woman's head rested on the table atop one of her stained glass windows. Shannon's heart raced at the sight. The woman had mentioned not feeling well earlier, but Shannon had no idea she'd felt this miserable. She should go home and have someone else man her booth if she felt this bad.

"Sunny?" Shannon rounded her table and approached Sunny's.

The woman remained still. Shannon gently reached forward and gently nudged her shoulder. "Sunny?"

Still no movement.

Shannon nudged her harder, and Sunny tumbled to the floor. Shannon didn't need to check Sunny's pulse to know the woman was dead.

# 2

At the sight of Sunny lying motionless on the floor, the buzz at the West Coast Art and Fine Craft Festival changed from one of cheerful excitement to horror in a matter of moments.

An ambulance arrived, followed by the police. The paramedics tried to resuscitate Sunny as they loaded her for transport, but Shannon knew it was too late.

She stood back, transfixed by shock, and watched as Sunny was wheeled to the waiting ambulance. The heavy doors slammed shut, and the ambulance tore out of the parking lot with its sirens screaming.

*How could this happen?* Shannon thought. She and Sunny had been laughing together less than an hour earlier ... and now the woman was dead? Sunny had mentioned not feeling well. Was that somehow connected with her death—an aneurism, perhaps?

Sunny was still young, probably in her mid-thirties. *Too young for a stroke*, thought Shannon. She wasn't an expert, but something about the circumstances reeked of foul play. People Sunny's age didn't often die of "natural" causes.

Her death apparently didn't sit right with the police either. Chief Jack Grayson's men cordoned off the area at ground zero—Sunny's booth—but they also instructed everyone to remain in the building until they could collect statements. That, Shannon knew, would take a while.

She'd gotten a good look at Sunny, sprawled white as a sheet on the gymnasium floor. There had been no obvious sign of foul play. No blood, no visible bruises. So how had Sunny died?

Shannon plopped into the chair behind her booth and ran her hand across her forehead. At the request of the show's organizer, Joyce had disappeared to help with crowd control, leaving Shannon alone with her tangled thoughts. What exactly was going on?

Confusion reigned on the showroom floor. People whispered and stared, likely theorizing about what could have happened. Mark Arnold, the show's organizer, appeared to be stressing over how the incident would affect the outcome of his show. No real surprise. That sounded like Mark. At least, it sounded like the Mark that Shannon had met.

"Did you see the discoloration of her nails?" A masculine voice drifted over the four-foot-tall curtain the police had set up around Sunny's booth.

Shannon's ears perked. Was that Chief Grayson talking? She felt like she should leave—like she shouldn't eavesdrop— yet she couldn't bring herself to move. The investigators at the other booth probably couldn't see her slouched in her chair. She leaned sideways, closer to the partition.

"That could be a sign of lead poisoning, or overexposure to lead, in the least."

Shannon recognized the voice; it was Grayson. *Lead poisoning?* Of course Sunny would have worked with lead in order to do her stained glass work. But surely a professional like Sunny wouldn't make amateurish mistakes. She would know how to handle chemicals like lead—would know to wear protective gear. There was no way Sunny had accidentally overexposed herself to it. Shannon worked with lead when she soldered her jewelry. One always had to be careful with it. It was the first thing a metalworker learned.

The chief's voice drifted over the partition again. "Metal poisoning can happen over a period of time. It slowly builds up so much that your body can't take it anymore. It might just be a coincidence that it happened today. Or lead poisoning might not have anything to do with her death at all."

As Shannon shifted in her chair, her hair caught on one of her necklaces hanging on a display rack, nearly knocking over the entire display. She caught the wooden stand and quietly straightened it without drawing attention to herself. Then she untangled her hair and slowly let out a breath, relieved she hadn't been caught red-handed, eavesdropping.

"Lead poisoning?" another voice asked. "From lead paint in her house, maybe?"

"Lead is everywhere," Grayson said. "It can remain in the dirt indefinitely. I'm not saying that's what killed her. It would be unusual, but not impossible. I'm surprised she wouldn't have noticed any symptoms earlier if it *was* lead poisoning. We'll know more after the autopsy."

*Lead poisoning.* If Sunny had taken the proper precautions while working on her pieces—and Shannon was sure that she had—then that left only one other option as to how she might have been overexposed.

Had someone poisoned Sunny and tried to make her death look like an accident? Shannon had no idea how anyone could do such a thing, but it seemed like a distinct possibility, given the circumstances.

If the police were right, and Sunny had died because of lead poisoning, then she had been murdered. Shannon felt sure of it.

Nausea roiled in Shannon's gut at the thought.

*       *       *

"Are you OK, Shannon?" Joyce peered at her from the other side of the booth, worry etched on her face. "You're looking awfully pale."

*Pale? Hadn't Sunny looked pale? Have I been poisoned too?*

Shannon shook her head. No, that was a ridiculous thought. It was just the shock of finding the dead body of her new friend that had made the blood drain from her face.

Shannon dropped her head into her hands. "I'm fine, Joyce, but thank you for asking. You're never prepared to see someone fall over dead, I suppose. I may be a tough Scot, but I'm not *that* tough."

"I hope you never get that tough. Speaking of which, where's that water girl when you need her?" Joyce craned her neck. "I'm going to find you something to drink. Maybe water will help. Be right back."

Various volunteers for the show had been delivering water to the exhibitors all day. It was a nice, thoughtful perk. All the artists had paid a hefty fee to participate, so every amenity helped.

As soon as her friend stepped away, Shannon let the facts surrounding Sunny's death sink in. One minute, her new friend had been alive and well, selling her artwork just as Shannon was selling hers. The next moment, she was gone. *Dead.*

A man cleared his throat above her. Shannon looked up to see Chief Grayson standing next to her table, staring at her.

"Shannon McClain. How is it you always seem to be at the wrong place at the wrong time?"

Shannon stood and straightened the oversized turquoise scarf she wore knotted around her neck. "This is my booth, Chief. I was merely sitting in the space designated as mine."

Chief Grayson was in his early fifties with balding brown hair and a slight paunch. A twinkle sparkled in his eyes. Shannon had worked with the chief in the past and knew him to be a fair man. He took his job seriously and didn't let emotions get in the way. He let the evidence lead him. Unfortunately, that evidence sometimes led him to places Shannon didn't want it to.

"I have a few questions for you," he said.

She nodded, trying to hide how shaken she was. "Go ahead. I want to find the person who murdered Sunny as much as you do."

His eyes narrowed. "No one said anything about murder."

Shannon wasn't one to pretend. "I overheard you talking. There's no way Sunny would have failed to wear a mask when she soldered with lead. She's an experienced professional."

"There are other ways to get lead poisoning, Shannon." Grayson's lips pulled in a tight line. "Besides, there's been no official pronouncement or cause of death yet. I'm going to have to ask you not to go spreading that rumor around."

Indignation spread through Shannon, from her toes all the way to the tips of her fingers, which were curled into tight balls as she placed her hands on her hips. "All I'm concerned about is figuring out what happened to her. If her death was a tragic accident or a unfortunate natural event, then so be it. But if it was anything more, I'd like to see justice served—as I'm sure you would."

The chief eyed her warily. He was a friend of Michael's, which made him soften somewhat toward Shannon. At least, that's the way it had seemed in the past. Right now, she felt like they were at odds, and she didn't know why.

"I assure you that justice will be served." Grayson shifted his weight and nodded toward Sunny's booth. "Now, what did you know about Ms. Davis? Did you talk to her much?"

Shannon fidgeted with the ends of her scarf. "She seemed to be a great person—really happy and down to earth. Of course, I only met her yesterday. I'm probably not the best person to ask."

"Did she mention anything that was wrong, or did she seem upset about anything today?"

Shannon shook her head as she tried to recall their conversation. "No, she seemed delighted to be here. She had customers coming here from up and down the Coast just to see her work. I know that the detail of her work has not gone unnoticed by industry professionals. She was one of the best."

"So I've heard," Grayson said. "Have you heard anyone speaking poorly of her? Any grumblings among the other artists here?"

Shannon shook her head again, her dangly earrings brushing her jaw. "No, I didn't hear anything. I can't imagine anyone having anything bad to say about the woman, God rest her soul."

"Is there anything else that stands out in your mind? I know you've got an eye for detail, Shannon."

That was probably about as close as the chief would ever come to complimenting her. "Sunny did mention that she wasn't feeling well earlier. She thought maybe she was coming down with a virus."

"Oh? Did she say anything specifically about *how* she felt bad?"

"A headache, I believe."

"Good to know." He nodded. "Thanks for your help. If you hear anything ...."

"I know the drill." In fact, Shannon knew it all too well. She'd been in this position far too many times in the past year. What did it say about her that whenever a mystery seemed to emerge, she was close by?

It must mean that she was supposed to lend a helping hand to those who couldn't speak for themselves any longer, she decided. She was well aware of her talents—jewelry making, managing her business, and tracking down criminals.

It was all in a day's work.

A new determination rose in Shannon as the chief walked away. She'd try not to jump the gun, as the saying went, but if the police declared that Sunny's death was due to accidental poisoning, then she might have to stick her nose into things. She couldn't believe Sunny would accidentally poison herself.

She wandered away from her booth and toward Joyce, who'd stopped to talk to fellow Purls of Hope member Melanie Burkhart on her way back to Shannon, cup of water in hand. The Purls were Shannon's dearest friends in the United States.

They met at least once a week to knit or work on other projects, oftentimes while sharing their lives with each other. Shannon felt she'd known them for much longer than the short time she actually had been in Apple Grove, Oregon.

In addition to designing floral arrangements at The Flower Pot, Melanie worked a few hours a week at Shannon's shop. Diagnosed with breast cancer two years earlier, Melanie's husband had left her, and he'd later turned up dead. Shannon was happy to say that the right person was now behind bars for his murder, and that Melanie was cancer free.

Shannon stopped beside her friends. Joyce handed her the water, and Melanie rubbed Shannon's arm with a slight frown on her face.

"I'm surprised to see you here," Shannon said to Melanie. "I didn't realize you were coming—or that the police were letting new people inside."

"I stopped by to see how things were going. Everyone in town is talking about how wonderful all of the art is here. I arrived right before the police, and I've been in the cafeteria since then." Her frown deepened, and she swallowed hard. "Is it true?"

"Is what true?" Shannon asked, wanting to know what Melanie had heard. She took a sip of her water.

"Was that stained glass artist *murdered*?"

Shannon sucked in a deep breath. The chief had told her not to spread that rumor. So where had her friend heard it? "Why would you think that?"

"People are figuring that all these police officers wouldn't be here if it *wasn't* murder." Melanie's eyes widened in surprise. "You know something, don't you?"

Shannon struggled for the right words. She hated keeping things from her friends. "I know her death is suspicious. That's all I can say."

Joyce shook her head. "It's such a shame. That woman was the most respected stained glass artist in the region—I daresay in the country. She didn't even need to do shows like this."

Shannon nodded. "We lost a great artist today, that's for sure. I can't imagine why anyone would want her dead."

Joyce peered at her intently. Her friend knew her too well. "You seem pretty convinced it was murder."

"I've been around it enough that I'm beginning to feel like an expert." Shannon glanced back at her booth. No one was there, but Sunny's booth was still a bustle of activity. Shannon hoped that all of the law enforcement officers were careful with Sunny's work as they examined the potential crime scene.

"You're pale," Joyce said. "Perhaps you should sit."

"I think I just need a bite to eat," Shannon said. "After all of the excitement, I forgot about lunch. Will you both be around for awhile?"

They nodded.

Shannon excused herself and went back over to her booth. She sat in her chair and reached under the table to get her lunch. The last thing she needed was to add low blood sugar to her already distressed state.

When her fingers failed to locate her lunch bag, she glanced at her purse and saw a note there. What was that? A request for some of her jewelry? Sometimes customers left notes when they didn't bring enough money to purchase items. But how had the note gotten on top of her purse? *Someone would have had to come around to the back of the booth to leave it here.*

Shannon's back muscles tightened. She grabbed the paper, unfolding the crisp square until it was flat. The words on the page caused her blood to run cold.

"It was murder."

# 3

Shannon clutched the cryptic note in her hand, her gaze frantically searching up and down the nearby aisles. *Who could have left this?* She could only assume that the note had been left during the brief period of time she had been talking to Melanie and Joyce. She'd already suspected foul play. Was the note proof that her suspicions were correct?

She scanned everything around her, looking for a clue or someone suspicious. Police officers, stressed-out artists, and people gawking with open curiosity—none of them looked like they'd left the note and run.

She forgot about her lunch and hurried back toward her friends, who still stood chatting in the aisle. "Did either of you notice anyone lingering around my booth while we were talking?" she asked.

"Only the police," Melanie said. "Why?"

She showed them the note. Their eyes widened as they read the words.

Joyce shook her head in what appeared to be disbelief. "This note is referring to Sunny? Someone knows she was murdered?"

"But who would know that?" asked Melanie.

Shannon's gaze roamed the floor again, but nothing unusual caught her eye. "Someone who saw something."

"But why would they leave that note for you?" Melanie asked. "Why not go to the police?"

"Maybe they're afraid of the police. A lot of people don't like talking to the police for one reason or another," Joyce said. Her voice sounded steady and strong, and left little room for argument.

"Especially because talking to the police might make you look guilty," Shannon said.

"Truer words were never spoken," Melanie said. Once falsely accused of her ex-husband's murder, she knew about that all too well.

"Maybe the person who wrote this note has heard about all the other crimes you've solved," Joyce speculated. She waved a finger at Shannon, her brightly painted fingernail shimmering beneath the fluorescent lights. "You're a lot less intimidating than the police."

Shannon shook her head. "I don't know what they want *me* to do with this information."

"If you ask me, it looks like they want you to find Sunny's killer." Joyce's raised eyebrows seemed suspended on her forehead. "Of course, that's just my opinion, and I'm known to have a lot of them."

Shannon let Joyce's words settle over her. Did someone really want her help? Sure, she'd helped solve a few other crimes in the past. She had an attention to detail that served her well in her art—and in her investigations. But that had almost gotten her killed a few times.

"The first thing I'm going to do is try and find the person who left this note and encourage them to go to the police. That would be the reasonable thing to do." Shannon's eyes sparkled. "You ladies want to help me?"

"You know it." Joyce nodded, excitement flashing in her eyes. "We Purls stick together."

"Count me in," Melanie said.

Shannon nodded, so thankful for of them. Their friendship meant the world to her. The women huddled together for a moment. "OK, let's split up. Between the three of us, let's see what we can dig up," Shannon said. "Someone here knows something. We just have to figure out who it is and what they know."

Melanie and Joyce nodded.

"We'll see what we can find out," Melanie said. "Maybe someone was mad at Sunny—mad enough to kill her."

"I'll stay and watch your booth, Shannon," Joyce said. "It's not smart to leave your jewelry unattended. Plus, I can keep my eye on everyone from there and nose around a bit. Maybe someone sitting in a nearby booth saw something."

Shannon smiled at her sweet friend. She'd been there for her more than once, and it wasn't something that had gone unnoticed. "Thanks. I appreciate it."

"You're better at digging up information than I am." Joyce winked.

"And you're the best salesperson I know, so I'd say it's a good trade."

Shannon turned and scanned the crowds. It was time to search for some answers.

*　　*　　*

The trio split up, but Shannon remained where she was, not sure where to start. There were so many faces at the show that she didn't recognize. *Which one of them might provide a clue?*

Sunny's work was much sought after. Could that be reason

enough for murder? There was one other stained glass artist at the show. Shannon decided it might be wise to learn more about Sunny's competition.

She made her way toward the woman's booth. Even from a distance, she could tell the woman's work was good, but it wasn't nearly as good as Sunny's. Sunny had had a natural talent; her work was high quality, yet it uniquely stood out among the competition.

Shannon paused a few steps from the stained glass artist's booth. The woman looked to be in her fifties with closely cropped hair, dyed an unnatural shade of orange, and artsy glasses. But what really caught Shannon's eye were her tears as she pulled a tissue from her purse. The woman was clearly upset. She must have known Sunny.

Shannon sighed. She wouldn't bother the woman—not now, at least. The woman had the right to mourn in private— as privately as one could at a busy arts and crafts show.

Shannon looked around, trying to decide what to do next. She could wander around, hoping to stumble onto a conversation that might help her, but that didn't seem like the best use of her time. *How am I going to figure out who left that note?*

She absently picked up a small, framed watercolor painting, trying not to look suspicious as she contemplated her next move. *How would someone poison a person with lead anyway? The killer couldn't simply slip it into the water ... could he? Might the culprit be a woman? She'd heard it said that poison was a woman's weapon.*

There was one thing Shannon was sure about: Someone at the show knew that Sunny had been murdered. The note was proof. If she could find whoever wrote it, then she could find answers.

"Shannon?" Michael's voice pulled her from her thoughts.

She placed the painting back onto the table and turned toward him. "What are you doing here again?" Not the warmest greeting she could have managed, but it was already out there.

"I was driving to another meeting when I saw all of the emergency vehicles out front. I had to make sure that you were—" He stopped mid-sentence.

*To make sure what?* Shannon thought. *To make sure that I was OK?*

Michael stepped back and looked around. "What happened?"

"You remember the nice stained glass artist in the booth beside mine? She fell over and died. Just like that. One minute, she was fine. The next, she was dead."

Michael frowned. "Any speculations as to the cause of death?"

"I overheard the police say it might be lead poisoning."

He raised his eyebrows. "Lead poisoning? That's an unusual one."

"But appropriate for a stained glass artist. That's what they use between their panes of glass. She worked around lead all the time." Shannon shook her head. "But she was a professional, Michael. There's no way she used it improperly."

Worry wrinkled the skin between his eyes. His hand went to her elbow. "Come on. You look like you could use something to eat. My treat."

"That's not necessary. I'm fine." She was supposed to be asking questions, trying to figure out who left the note. But before she could protest further, Michael led her toward the door.

"I insist. Besides, I hear they have killer cheesecake."

He knew her well. She was always a sucker for cheese-cake—though she could do without the "killer" part. But it would be nice to step away from all the craziness for a moment and clear her head.

They left the gym area and walked toward the cafeteria. The scents of freshly baked bread, herb-seasoned soup, and coffee floated around her, making her stomach growl. Her appetite was still squelched from the turmoil, but Michael was right. She needed to eat.

Shannon knew what the main topic of conversation was among the patrons gathered at the tables—Sunny. Shannon wanted to tell Michael about the note. He was always a great sounding board when it came to solving mysteries, and his work as a detective allowed him to add invaluable insight.

Finally at the head of the line, Shannon ordered crab bisque, which was served in a crusty, warm bread bowl. Michael got the same. He balanced their tray in his hands as they found a table in the corner. She sat on a twisty stool attached to a collapsible table, feeling for a moment like a schoolgirl again. Despite the grim circumstances, she couldn't help but let out a soft sigh and twist back and forth, burning off a little nervous energy.

Michael's eyes sparkled from across the table. Shannon figured Michael had been one of those guys in high school that all the girls wanted to eat lunch with. She'd been her own person, even as a teen, preferring to hang out with the creative types more than the athletes or the "cool" crowd.

She had unscrewed the cap on a bottle of water and was taking a long sip when a conversation at the table beside them caught her ear. Shannon turned slightly to glance at the woman who was talking.

"Two ladies were fighting over one of her pieces earlier. Do you think one of them could have killed her?" The tiny woman with gray hair took a bite of a gooey brownie.

The other woman, about the same age but bigger and less fragile looking, scoffed. "Over a stained glass window? That sounds like nonsense. I bet it was an old boyfriend or something. Aren't they always the guilty ones?"

"I think it'll turn out to be a less obvious choice. Like one of her customers. Or maybe she was running a scam, and she didn't handcraft any of her pieces after all."

The other woman's eyes lit up. "Maybe she ordered them from China! Wouldn't that be quite the scandal?"

Both of the women laughed, and as they continued to eat their dessert, their conversation turned to the weather.

"Are you really giving any credit to what those women are saying?" Michael whispered.

Shannon shrugged, knowing she'd been caught. Being guilty of eavesdropping was the least of her worries at the moment. "I was just listening."

He leaned closer, resting his elbows on the table. "You're not planning to get involved, are you? This seems like a terrible tragedy, but not a murder."

Shannon pursed her lips. "I don't know. I mean, the police can handle everything, I suppose."

"Exactly." Michael leaned back as if satisfied.

She locked gazes with him. "Asking a few innocent questions here and there can't hurt."

The satisfied look on his face disappeared. "Shannon ..."

She raised her brows. "What? I know a lot about art. I feel like my expertise here could be utilized."

Michael took a spoonful of his soup and then wiped his mouth with a paper napkin. "Do you sell lead in your store?"

"Yes, as a matter of fact, I do." Ideas began whirling in Shannon's brain. "It actually comes spooled."

"And how does one use it when creating stained glass art?"

"They cut out the pieces of glass and usually place them on top of a pattern." She moved her hands around the table, acting out each part of the process. "They place the spooled lead—it's called lead came—between the pieces and then solder them together."

"And how would one get lead poisoning from doing that?"

"Either from the fumes or the dust. When the solder is melted, it puts off toxic fumes. That's why a lot of stained glass artists now use copper instead."

He raised an eyebrow as he ripped off a piece of his bread bowl. "But not Sunny?"

She shook her head. "No. Sunny was telling me yesterday that she liked to do things the old-fashioned way. She liked the patina from the lead and thought it looked better if she used lead came. She also used twisted lead to frame up her pieces. It took a lot more time to make the ornamental pieces, but customers—and critics—noticed."

"You don't think there's a chance she mishandled the lead?"

Shannon shook her head. "Absolutely not. Sunny was too seasoned a craftsperson to make an amateur mistake like that."

Michael slowly nodded. "If that's the case, then it only leaves one other alternative."

Shannon met his gaze. "She was poisoned."

"Poisoning with lead would probably have to be done gradually," he said. "This means the guilty party is likely someone close to her."

"Makes sense."

"The question is, where would someone get lead to do that? You can't exactly bottle the fumes and make someone breathe them."

Shannon's mind raced through the possibilities. "I suppose someone could take those came strips and make dust from them. It would be a long, drawn-out process, but it could be done."

"Has anyone purchased spooled lead from your store lately?"

That was a great question, but Shannon wasn't sure of the answer. "I'll have to check my records. Better yet, I'll call Essie and have her check since I don't know when I'll make it back the store." Essie Engleman managed the Paisley Craft Market for Shannon.

"That would be a good place to start," Michael said. "I would say it's not likely that any lead used to poison Sunny would have come from a local source. But Grayson may be asking you that very question in the near future, so it wouldn't hurt to have the answer ready." His voice sounded stern, which caused a realization to swell in Shannon.

She sat up straighter, her eyes widening. "You think it was murder too, don't you?"

"Can't say. There still isn't any hard evidence," Michael said. "But based on what you've told me, I agree that some-one with Sunny's expertise wouldn't make a careless mis-take like that."

Shannon took her first spoonful of soup. Creamy warmth hit her taste buds and made her close her eyes in delight. It was delicious—just what she needed to drive away the chill that emanated from her core. Michael had agreed that Sunny's death was suspicious. Her instinct had been right.

For the rest of the meal, Michael tried to distract her by talking about everything except Sunny. She appreciated his efforts, but it didn't work. Nothing could erase the mental image of Sunny lying dead on the floor.

When they finished, Shannon wiped her mouth and nodded toward the showroom area. Her stomach felt full, and her heart felt heavy. "I'm going to head back. Would you like to join me?"

He nodded. "I'll stop in and say hello to the chief, to see if he wants to talk about the case."

Michael had been a police detective in Portland before his wife was murdered by a drug cartel hit man in retaliation for his work in the narcotics division. After that, Michael had steered clear of close relationships, fearing that someone he cared about would get hurt again because of him.

Shannon stopped at the information booth near the front door of the gym. Margaret, a member of the local artists guild, was handing out flyers there. Guild members had agreed to help with the show in return for a small percentage of the profits for the guild.

"I'll meet you back here," Michael said, his gaze fixed on Chief Grayson.

Shannon nodded and sidled up to Margaret. In her role as a volunteer, she'd probably talked to almost everyone who'd come and gone since the start of the show. That meant that she could be a wealth of information.

"How's it going, Margaret?"

"What a morning, huh?" The woman's voice held the tinge of sorrow. She held a stack of flyers with maps of the showroom floor in one of her hands. The pages had wrinkles in them, as if Margaret had been gripping them too hard.

"You can say that again." Shannon tried to keep her voice casual. "Have you heard any updates about … what happened?"

Margaret shook her head. Her coiffed hair didn't move an inch. "Rumors are flying that she was poisoned. Isn't that tragic?"

"More than tragic. I talked to Sunny earlier, and she seemed like the nicest woman."

Margaret gripped the maps again, crumpling the papers in her hand. "I thought so too. She had talent and heart. I can't say that about everyone I meet at these shows."

"I can't imagine who would do such a terrible thing to such a sweet woman," Shannon said. "Can you?"

Margaret looked around before stepping closer and lowering her voice. "I don't know, but I can say this: This morning, before everyone arrived, I overheard Sunny and Mark Arnold arguing about something. I couldn't hear what it was, but their conversation was heated, to say the least. Mark's always had a bit of a temper, and he hasn't been pleasant to work with. In fact, I doubt I'll ever volunteer to help him again. None of the guild members will."

"He has a temper, you say?" Shannon had seen Mark arguing with the woodcarver earlier in the day too. It seemed that the man had been doing a lot of fussing lately.

Margaret nodded, her voice turning ominous. "A nasty temper that makes me wonder what he'd be capable of if he got angry enough."

Shannon sucked in a breath as Margaret's implication washed over her.

*Did Mark Arnold get angry enough to poison someone?*

# — 4 —

Shannon caught a glimpse of Michael chatting with Chief Grayson as she made her way back to her own booth. Their conversation looked serious, based on the way the two of them talked quietly without a hint of a smile.

She approached her table where Joyce and Melanie huddled together, whispering. She didn't waste any time with pleasantries. "Did you all learn anything new?"

They each shook their heads, indicating they'd hit dead ends. "No one saw anyone other than police officers near your booth," Joyce said. "I even offered a free gourmet cupcake as a bribe for information."

Melanie nodded in agreement. "No one I talked to saw anything either."

Shannon bit her lip, thinking. Everyone was probably concentrating on other things after Sunny's body was discovered, she supposed, like watching as the body was carried away. The person who'd left the note probably knew that. His or her timing had been impeccable. "What about information on Sunny? Did you learn anything on that front?"

"Everyone said that Sunny was well loved," Melanie said. "They can't imagine anyone wanting to hurt her. It's the same story over and over."

Joyce nodded. "Some of these people have worked

numerous shows with Sunny. They all said Sunny's always been nothing but pleasant—that she lived up to her name."

Melanie pointed to the egg painter across the aisle. "That lady told me that a lot of people, when they reach the level of success that Sunny had, become difficult or arrogant. Not Sunny. She was still as down to earth as ever."

Shannon put a hand on her hip, trying to cut through her emotions and think logically. "Let's be honest. Shows like this one are cutthroat. Everyone wants to get in. For some of these people, getting into a show like this could mean the difference between paying their bills and going broke. An artist without a venue to sell her work is called poor. That might be reason enough for murder."

"I can't argue with that," Joyce said. "There's a reason I'm a baker and not a full-time artist. Besides, isn't money always a motive?"

"Money or love," Shannon said. "Sometimes both."

Melanie turned toward Shannon. "How about you? Did you find out anything?"

Shannon nodded, trying to mentally wade through everything she'd learned. "I learned that Sunny had a big fight with Mark Arnold this morning before the doors opened."

"He's the one who organized this show," Melanie said, her eyebrows knitted together. "And he's the president of the Artists Guild of the Northwest. Do you know what the fight was about?"

Shannon shook her head. "Only that it was heated."

"Mark nearly bit off my head when I first got here," Joyce said. "He told me I was supposed to be helping, not standing around talking. I can understand why people don't care for him."

Melanie looked at Shannon and said, "Maybe we should go talk to Mark."

"That might not be a bad idea." Shannon caught herself glancing over at Michael as she said the words. She knew he wouldn't approve, but she was a grown woman and had to make her own choices. Finding out if a fellow artisan had been murdered was important to her. Besides, asking a few questions didn't mean she was engaging in a full-scale investigation. It meant she was being a friend.

Melanie stepped forward, looping her arm through Shannon's. "I'll go with you."

"I'll continue to man the booth." Joyce gave a mock salute.

Shannon's heart swelled. She'd truly been blessed with great friends in the short time she'd been in Apple Grove. Could she entertain the idea of leaving all of her new friends? Could she leave her new home and move to Chicago? The town and the people of Apple Grove were as inviting as warm rhubarb pie on a cold day—and a person didn't find that kind of sweetness every day. Rupert Murphy's offer fluttered through her mind again. Had it just been this morning when she'd spoken with him? It seemed like weeks had passed since their exchange.

Shannon shook off the thought and focused on the task at hand. The two ladies began to meander through the crowds, searching for Mark. Since the doors had opened again, and most of the police were gone, business had begun to pick up.

Shannon sighed. *How quickly the loss of life could be forgotten.* Was it macabre curiosity, or were people already thinking about their Christmas lists?

Melanie leaned in close and lowered her voice. "I see Michael stopped by again."

Shannon nodded. "He did. He happened to be driving past and saw that something was going on."

"And then he had to stop by and check on you." Melanie cast a knowing glance her way as they sidestepped a crowd gathered around a landscape photographer's booth. "You know it's true, Shannon. He's your proverbial Prince Charming, always riding in when you need him."

Shannon couldn't deny that Michael had risked his life to save hers on more than one occasion. "We're friends. That's enough, isn't it?"

"When you find a good man, you should hold onto him."

Shannon shook her head. "You can't hold onto someone who's not yours."

"What's the story with that Hunter fellow? He's been hanging around quite a bit."

"He's a friend too. We're supposed to have dinner together sometime this week," Shannon confessed.

Melanie's head swiveled toward Shannon, and her mouth dropped open. "Like a date?"

Shannon shrugged, still keeping an eye out for Mark Arnold. "I suppose you could call it that."

"Does Michael know?"

"I doubt it. Why would he care?"

Melanie gave Shannon a knowing look. "You know why."

Shannon shook her head as she dodged a group of women who'd obviously come to the show together. They walked in a big cluster, laughing and trying to read a wrinkled map of exhibitors.

"Let's not talk about my love life right now—or the lack thereof," Shannon said. Thankfully, her cellphone rang and saved her from the conversation. She glanced at the screen before answering it. It was Essie, her manager at the Paisley Craft Market.

"I heard what happened." Essie was one to cut to the chase.

Shannon stepped away from Melanie for a moment. "It got back to you already?"

Essie snorted. "This is Apple Grove. News travels quickly."

"I'd say so. Listen, Essie, I'm glad you called. I need to know if anyone has purchased lead came strips from us lately, the kind you use to make stained glass art."

"The spooled lead? What would that have to do with this?"

"No one knows for sure yet," Shannon said. "We'll have to wait for a toxicology screen of Sunny's blood, but I overheard someone say that her body displayed indications of lead poisoning."

"You think someone poisoned that poor lady using a product from our store?" Essie's voice caught. "That *we* may have sold it to a murderer?"

"It's just a lead that needs to be checked out. I'm trying to rule out every possibility."

"So you're on the case? You do have quite the reputation for solving crime now."

Shannon stared at the people milling around in the distance, the same nervous chatter buzzing through the crowds. "No one would hire me, but I suspect the police will ask about the lead came. It can't hurt to have the information ready."

"Sure thing. Give me one minute."

Shannon continued to scan the crowds as she waited. She saw nothing suspicious. A few people had begun to shop again, but the overhead music still hadn't come back on. The air in the place had changed. Gone was the jovial spirit from earlier, and in its place was a certain tension.

Essie came back on the line. "It looks like we've sold two spools of the product in the past month. They were to Dina Miller and ..."

Shannon's back muscles tightened as she pushed herself away from the wall and stood ramrod straight in anticipation of the next name. "Who is it, Essie?"

"Well, it looks like Hunter Banks bought some too."

"*Hunter?*" Shannon blinked. Why in the world would Hunter Banks buy lead came? He certainly didn't seem like the artsy type. He was a marine biologist in town on a grant from the National Science Foundation. "You're sure?"

"Positive."

"OK. Thanks for the information, Essie. Call me if you need anything."

Stunned, Shannon joined her friends, who were now standing at her booth. She shared the new information with them.

"Hunter?" Melanie leaned closer and lowered her voice. "Do you really think he had something to do with this?"

Shannon's heart sank. She wished she could offer a quick negative response, but she couldn't. "I have no idea what to think at this point. He is new in town. He's never expressed any kind of interest in stained glass—at least not to me."

Joyce nodded somberly. "I've got to admit, that's sending up a red flag—but maybe he has a logical explanation."

Shannon bit her lip. It sent up a red flag for her also. The first day she'd met Hunter, the day he'd shown up at her store looking lost and in need of directions to the rental agency, he'd seemed so out of place. She would've bet he'd never set foot in a craft store before that day.

"Look who just walked in," Melanie said, nodding toward the main entrance.

Shannon followed her gaze and saw Mark Arnold, his hair rumpled as if he'd been running his hands through it, and his entire body rigid. Was that what the stress of killing someone would do to a person?

She decided it was time they had a talk.

*     *     *

"You think *I* killed Sunny?" Mark Arnold's eyes looked like they might pop out of his head. His tiny round glasses only seemed to magnify their saucerlike quality. The man was tall, in his mid-forties, and had thinning light brown hair. "What reason could I possibly have for doing that?"

"That's *not* what I said. I simply asked if you know anything about her death." Shannon stepped closer, realizing that several people near them on the showroom floor could easily overhear the conversation. "But since you jumped to that conclusion, you tell us."

Melanie nodded and crossed her arms.

Mark looked around before responding. "Look, it could be really bad for business if anyone overhears this conversation." Panic seemed to lace his words.

*Precisely,* Shannon thought. There was nothing like pressure to get a person to tell the truth. "The sooner you talk, the sooner this conversation will be over."

Shannon could see a vein pulsating at his temple. This seemed to be a man on the edge. But was that just his personality, or was it because he'd done something horrible?

He stepped closer. "Let's go into the hallway."

Shannon wasn't sure it was a good idea to go anywhere with him—even the hallway. But Melanie was with her. As long as they didn't go anywhere too secluded, they should be fine. She glanced at Melanie before nodding.

They left the gym and stepped into the hallway, finding a nook in the corner away from the crowds.

Mark didn't waste any time once they were out of ear-shot of the masses. "Look, it's like this. Sunny and I *did* have an argument this morning."

"About what?"

"Sunny didn't appreciate the way I do business." The vein at his temple continued to bulge.

"Meaning?"

Mark's neck appeared to tighten again. He ran a nervous finger around his collar. "Meaning that she thought I was rude and overbearing, and that I turned people off."

*And all of that is true,* Shannon thought.

Melanie took her turn in the detective's seat. "*That* must have really angered you."

"Not enough that I would kill someone!" He threw his hands in the air, and a few people in the distance stopped to stare. Then he gulped a deep breath, as if to calm himself before continuing. "That's ridiculous."

Shannon wasn't ready to let the conversation drop. "You and Sunny have done several shows together. You would've had the perfect opportunity to poison her—gradually."

"Poison her?" Mark pulled a handkerchief from his pocket and ran it over his forehead. "Is that what they're saying happened? She was poisoned?"

Melanie shrugged. "That's the rumor."

"That's awful, but I'll say it again. I would never do something like that." He swept a hand over his face, and Shannon saw his fingers tremble. "Look, Sunny brings a lot of business to my shows. A *lot* of business. People love her work. That's one of the reasons she was so upset with me. We *have* worked together several times, but I still make her jump through all of the same hoops that I make everyone else jump through."

*Where is he going with this?* Shannon wondered. "Why did you do that?"

"It's only fair. Do you know how much flack I would get if the other exhibitors here found out I gave her special treatment?"

Shannon could understand that, though she hated to admit it. Mark was downright prickly, and his temperament seemed to lean toward neurotic. But he said he tried to treat everyone fairly, even one of the show's brightest stars. Was there another side to Sunny that Shannon hadn't seen in their brief encounters?

Mark threw back his head and sucked in another deep breath, as if practicing a technique taught to him by a therapist. When he straightened again, his gaze appeared steadier. "If you want to talk to someone who might have the answers, you should talk to Alana Golden."

Shannon tilted her head. "Who's she?"

He nodded in the distance. "She's the other stained glass artist. She and Sunny are—*were*, I should say—friends, so she might know if anyone had been giving Sunny a hard time."

"Isn't it unusual to have two stained glass artists at the show?"

"It only turned out that way because someone else had to drop out at the last minute. Sunny asked me—begged practically—if I'd take Alana instead. I guess she's hurting for business."

Melanie shook her head. "Sunny asked you to allow the competition into the show?"

"There's really no competition," Mark said. "Alana does good work for smaller art shows. But her work dims in comparison to Sunny's. I mean, who would buy her stuff over Sunny's?"

Shannon was trying to follow his logic. "Why did you let her in then?"

He shook his head as if his neuroses were trying to rise to the surface again. "Sunny was adamant that Alana be added. It was the last minute, and I didn't have time to find someone else to fill the space. Occupied space is everything here." Mark shrugged. "I asked Alana if she wanted to be part of the show."

Shannon nodded. She knew exactly whom she needed to talk to next.

# — 5 —

Shannon dragged herself out of bed the next morning after a sleepless night. She threw on her robe, her head pounding from lack of rest, and went downstairs to find some caffeine.

The previous evening, she hadn't been able to stop thinking about Sunny and her death. Her thoughts had bounced between Mark Arnold's claims and images of Sunny working without protective gear.

Shannon knew the case wasn't really any of her business. She wondered if she should drop it and leave the investigating to the authorities.

*Why am I having so much trouble letting this go?* Was it because Sunny had been so kind—had seemed like a kindred spirit? Or was it that Shannon had been the one to find her and call the police? She didn't know.

She poured herself a cup of coffee, freshly brewed by Deborah Waters, her live-in cook, and then sat on a barstool at the counter. She glanced around the kitchen, still awestruck by the state-of-the-art space. Before her grandmother, Victoria Paisley, had died, she'd refurbished the room with granite counters, tile flooring, two ovens, and practically every other gadget that could be imagined. Off the kitchen were a glassed-in garden terrace, a breakfast room, and a formal dining room.

Her great-grandparents had built the Mediterranean-style mansion in the 1930s. It stood three stories tall and was flanked on two corners with turrets. If Shannon climbed to the very top floor of Paisley mansion, she could catch a glimpse of the ocean. Behind the mansion were a small lake, gardens, and a summer house.

She'd thought she would feel small in such a large house, but the place now felt like home. Personal touches from her grandmother gave Shannon insights into her family history. Living in such a grand house hadn't been a remote possibility for Shannon a year ago, when she'd been living in her little cottage in Wainscott, Scotland.

Then she'd received a letter from an attorney informing her of her unexpected inheritance from a grandmother she'd never known. Funny how the events of one day could drastically alter the course of one's life.

As she took another sip of coffee, her mind wandered back to Sunny. It couldn't hurt to ask a few questions. After all, she'd probably get answers more quickly than the chief would. She would merely appear like the unassuming crafter who'd found Sunny, and who was trying to deal with her shock. People would be more likely to open up to her.

In that way, she'd be helping. She suspected Chief Grayson and Michael would disagree with her assessment, however.

She yawned and poured herself another cup of coffee. A glance at her watch showed that she only had twenty more minutes before she needed to leave in order to get to the festival on time. She put one of Deborah's homemade cinnamon rolls on a plate and stuck it in the microwave for a few seconds. Shannon really didn't want to eat, but the warm roll would give her the sustenance she needed to begin what was sure to be a busy Saturday at the show.

She'd only taken two bites when her cellphone rang. It was her daughter, Lara. A wave of delight washed over her. Hearing from one of her teenage twins was always the highlight of her day. Lara and her brother, Alec, were in college now. It still seemed hard to believe that they were already old enough to live on their own.

"Hey, sweetie," Shannon said. "How are you? How are your classes going?"

"Fine. Lots of interesting people here, Mum. I like Portland a lot." Lara filled her in on everything that had happened in her life since the last time they'd talked. "I miss you, Mum, and I guess I'm a little homesick. If you would cook stovies for me for me the next time I'm in, it would probably help."

Shannon smiled. "I'd love to. I'll even cook you fish and chips, and wrap them in newspaper." She was so glad that Lara and Alec had transferred to a university in the States and now lived less than an hour away. They were the center of her world since her husband, John, had been killed in a car accident in Scotland three years before she'd moved to Apple Grove.

"That sounds brilliant," Lara said. "I'm thinking about heading your way next weekend for a visit. Would that be OK?"

"That would be more than OK. I'd love to see you." Shannon thought the visit might help take her mind off Sunny, as well.

"You're the best, Mum. Thanks."

Shannon was still smiling as she hung up. She only wished that John could see the twins now. He'd be so proud of how they were turning out.

She had spent so much of her life taking care of the kids; it had been quite an adjustment when they'd left for their first year of college at St. Andrews University. But then she'd learned of her mysterious inheritance and had moved to Apple Grove, to the 15-acre property, and had taken over her grandmother's craft market. It turned out that busyness was a fairly effective cure for empty-nest syndrome.

Shannon took a deep breath and forced her thoughts to turn to her present dilemma—Rupert Murphy's offer. She found her purse and dug out the envelope that Rupert had left her. She tugged the seal open, pulled out the papers, and began leafing through them. The pay he offered was great—more than great, actually. And she'd get ample vacation time and bonuses, and free rein to design her jewelry line. The offer was almost too good to be true.

Her eyes stopped at one of the stipulations. *Move to Chicago.* Just as she had feared.

Should she even consider the offer? Financially, she was set. She didn't need the money that a better, more prestigious job would bring. But everything wasn't about money. Having her pieces featured in stores across the country, as Rupert had suggested, would be … thrilling. Her name could become famous in the world of jewelry design.

Should she "shoot for the stars"—perhaps give Rupert a call and explore the possibility of doing something bigger than what she was doing in Apple Grove?

Michael's face flashed through her mind. No, she couldn't let him affect the outcome of her decision. He'd made it clear that he wasn't interested in being anything more than friends.

She bit into her cinnamon roll, wondering what it would be like to start over again. Giving herself a mental shake, she took a sip of her coffee. She shouldn't even consider it—her new life in Apple Grove was wonderful.

* * *

An hour later, Shannon wandered into the arts and crafts show and stopped near the door. She waved hello to Margaret, who was once again handing out flyers, before surveying the gym. Everything appeared to be back to normal. People chatted casually, and exhibitors straightened their booths with care. It was as if the horrific events of the previous day had never happened. Life went on, Shannon supposed, no matter how hard that was to swallow at times.

Her gaze stopped at Alana. She hadn't had a chance to talk with the woman yesterday. Alana's apparent consuming grief at Sunny's death had postponed the conversation that she was determined to have today. She also needed to talk to Hunter. Why in the world would he have purchased lead came from her shop? It was only a matter of time before the chief asked her about the purchases, and she'd have no choice but to tell him the truth.

She waved hello to several people as she passed, observing them carefully for any indication that they might know something or show the faintest sign of a tinge of guilt. She perceived none—only exhibitors ready for customers, with all their wares proudly displayed.

Shannon paused at Sunny's booth. Her work had been packed into boxes, and the booth sat empty. It was almost as if she had never been there. But Shannon certainly hadn't been able to forget her presence, nor would she until she had some answers.

Spotting two women waiting for her at her own booth, Shannon realized she needed to quicken her pace. She plastered on a smile as she hurried to the other side of her table and dropped her purse to the ground. "Good morning, ladies!"

The older of the two women smiled. "Early birds get the worms, isn't that right? We got here as soon as the doors opened. We were afraid something had happened to you too."

Shannon's throat went dry, and she began pulling out her jewelry pieces and placing them on their displays. "No, I'm fine."

The woman at least had the decency to blush. "I'm sorry. I shouldn't have said that. But I heard about the incident yesterday, and it's just terrible. Do you have any idea what happened to that poor woman?"

Shannon shook her head and placed a box of bracelets, smartly laid out on a black velvet backdrop, on the table. As she shifted to grab another box, something on the floor beneath her table caught her eye.

*Another cryptic note?*

Shannon resisted the urge to reach down and swoop it up right then and there, although that was exactly what she wanted to do. "I haven't heard anything definitive."

"Is it true that you found her body?" the second woman asked.

Shannon nodded, the memory forever stained in her mind. She absently began to straighten her displays. "I did. It was terrible."

"Land sakes! Don't make her rehash it, Sandy," the first woman scolded. She held up a necklace. "This is beautiful. I'd like to buy it. In fact, all of your work is gorgeous."

Shannon forced a smile. "Thank you. I appreciate that."

"I heard about you from a friend of a friend a few months ago. I've been anxious to check out your work for myself since then. When I found out you'd be attending this show, I knew I had to come."

"I'm flattered." Shannon hadn't believed Rupert when he said word of mouth about her work had been increasing. Not because she was insecure; she knew her work was good. But she'd simply had no idea that the word had traveled.

"You own that craft store in town. Is that right?" Sandy asked.

"I do." Shannon nodded, fondly picturing Paisley Craft Market & Artist Lofts. The place made crafters' dreams come true. On the second floor of the shop, she rented space to artists to use as studios, or to set up mini-stores or as a place to give lessons. She was almost as proud of the store as she was of her jewelry designs.

"I've heard wonderful things about the store," Sandy said. "And the coffee shop you have attached to it. Espresso Yourself, I believe it's called? Just brilliant."

The women continued to talk for several more minutes. Normally Shannon wouldn't have minded, but today the mysterious piece of paper on the floor beckoned for her attention. As soon as her customers left, she reached down and grabbed it. But before she could unfold the neatly pressed edges, another customer appeared at her table.

Shannon licked her lips, feeling especially impatient. Her curiosity had her on edge. However, the last thing she wanted was for someone to see her reading it and ask questions. She'd just have to wait. With a sigh, she stuffed the paper into the pocket of her sweater.

"Shannon McClain?" The customer kept her focus on Shannon, completely ignoring the jewelry.

"Yes." A sense of foreboding came over Shannon, and she got the feeling the woman wasn't doing early Christmas shopping like the other patrons in the gym. "How can I help you?"

"I'm Roberta Wilkerson. I'm a reporter for *The Artist's Touch*. Perhaps you've heard of us. We're the leading art magazine in the country, and we just went all digital."

Shannon straightened and grasped the reporter's outstretched hand. "It's a pleasure to meet you." She quickly appraised the tall, thirty-something woman. Dressed in a charcoal-color suit, with her stark black hair cut in a sharp wedge, Roberta looked like she could've stepped off the pages of a fashion magazine.

Roberta leaned in close. "Listen, I've heard a lot about your jewelry designs, and I was hoping that you might be interested in giving me an interview. I'd bring a photographer out and snap a few pictures."

"Me?"

The woman smiled, and that one action made her seem more approachable by leaps and bounds. "Yes, you. We like to highlight the best artists from across the country."

"And you think I fall into that category?" Shannon waited for lightning to strike; she'd never expected when she entered the art show that her work would be highlighted this much.

Roberta smiled again. "I appreciate your humility, but about that interview ... we actually had to cut our feature story for our upcoming issue, and I'm looking for someone who's available for a quick turnaround. Even though we're completely digital now, we still get a lot of exposure."

Shannon nodded, coming back to earth. Despite the attention, she had to remain grounded. "Sure thing. Just let me know when."

"How about Monday? We could meet somewhere neutral, or I could swing by your place—give our readers a glimpse of the 'behind-the-scenes' you."

"My place it is."

Shannon gave Roberta her address, and the reporter agreed to stop by around five o'clock on Monday. Excitement rushed through Shannon. *Maybe something good will come out of this show after all.*

Not that the good could possibly outweigh the bad.

The stream of customers continued to be steady. Finally, at eleven thirty, Shannon got a break. She pulled the note from her pocket and quickly read it.

The words on the page made her suck in a sharp breath: "Don't give up. Sunny needs your help. Keep asking questions."

\*     \*     \*

Shannon surveyed the crowds. *Who left this note?* It confirmed to her that someone at the show knew what had happened. It also seemed like there was a pretty good chance that the person who killed Sunny was somehow associated with the show. That's what her gut told her at least.

She wondered if the coroner had officially confirmed Sunny's cause of death yet. Perhaps when Grayson called to ask her if she sold any type of lead product at the craft market, she'd ask him. And she felt certain that he'd be calling. He was usually very thorough in his investigations.

Shannon spotted Mark talking to someone in the distance. As usual, the conversation looked heated. There was something about the man that Shannon didn't like. And apparently, she wasn't the only one who felt that way. And if he could get under the skin of someone as sweet as Sunny, then he could annoy anyone.

Shannon spotted Alana near her booth. The woman still appeared upset. From where Shannon stood, Alana's eyes looked red-rimmed. Shannon watched as the woman daintily wiped her nose with a tissue.

Joyce strode toward Shannon, her smile matching the glimmering beads on the collar of her shirt. After they hugged, Shannon asked, "Could you sit in my booth for a moment? I need a quick break."

"Of course. That's what I'm here for."

Shannon gave her another hug. "You're the best."

Walking toward Alana, Shannon wondered how she would start the conversation. *How can I ask her about something so horrible without seeming insensitive ... or just plain nosy?*

"Shannon!"

Her head swung toward the voice. Margaret motioned her over to the information booth. Did she have news about Sunny's death? Shannon hated to put off talking to Alana again, but Margaret seemed excited about something. Perhaps she had important information to share.

"Is everything OK?" Shannon asked, joining Margaret at the booth.

Margaret smiled. "Better than OK, but I realized I didn't ask you a very important question yesterday."

"Oh?"

"Would you like to join our local artists guild?"

Shannon's hope faded. It wasn't exactly what she'd wanted to hear. She bit the inside of her lip as the woman continued to try to convince her that the benefits of membership were worth the cost. As Margaret talked, Shannon's gaze traveled across the floor to Alana, the woman she desperately wanted to speak with.

*What did Alana just slip inside her purse?*

It looked like a clear plastic container full of a powdery-gray substance. Glitter? Or something more deadly—something like lead dust?

But that didn't make sense. The lead that stained glass artists used was spooled like ribbon.

As Margaret chattered on, Shannon considered the possibility that a vilely determined killer might make lead dust from the spooled ribbon and use it to poison someone.

*Could it be?*

# — 6 —

"Sorry to interrupt," Joyce said, her voice playful and light. "But that nice woman standing at your booth has a question about a necklace I can't answer."

Shannon pulled her gaze off Alana and saw her friend's eyes dancing with amusement.

"Please excuse me," Shannon said to Margaret. "I'll give the membership some serious thought."

She and Joyce hurried away.

"I could've helped the customer myself," Joyce whispered. "But you looked like you needed an escape."

"Thanks. I owe you one." Shannon relayed what she'd seen Alana doing. "What other kinds of gray powder are there?"

Joyce shrugged. "Eye shadow?"

"That would be a logical explanation, but the container looked too long and deep to be makeup. Any other ideas?"

"Chalk powder? Some artists use it on ceramics or paintings."

Shannon nodded thoughtfully. "Perhaps"

"Why don't you ask Alana? That is, after you talk to this customer," Joyce said, nodding toward a blonde standing patiently by Shannon's table. "You know what they say about customer service: It's everything."

Shannon smiled. "I couldn't agree more."

Talking to Alana would have to wait ... again. But Shannon's list of questions for her was growing exponentially.

She went back to her booth, where a woman, wearing an oversized hat brimmed with sparkles, stood. The woman wore several pieces of jewelry, beautiful jewelry at that—she obviously liked bling.

"Are you the mastermind behind these creations?" The woman fingered a necklace featuring a cascade of semiprecious stones that looked fit for royalty.

"Guilty as charged," Shannon said, keeping her tone light.

"You're good," the woman muttered. "I'm a bit of a jewelry connoisseur, and I know talent when I see it. You, my dear, have got talent."

Shannon grinned as she slipped to the other side of her table. "Thank you. I appreciate that. I don't do very many shows like this."

"I think you're good enough to go beyond these rinky-dink shows. I can't believe I'm saying this, but I think you could even get away with raising your prices. People would pay a lot for work like this."

Shannon's conversation with Rupert danced through her mind again. Should she take heed? Was this a sign that she was destined for bigger and better things?

She shook off the thought. She liked her simple little life in Apple Grove. Bigger did not always equate with better.

"I appreciate that. I really do."

"Think about it. But before you raise your prices, I'll take those two necklaces." The woman laughed.

Shannon wrapped the pieces in tissue paper and placed them in a brown paper bag while Joyce handled the money. The woman smiled widely before grabbing a few business cards to give to her friends.

"Have a lovely day," Shannon said to the woman and watched her walk away.

No sooner had the woman wandered off than a large bouquet of daisies was thrust into Shannon's face.

"For you," a deep voice said from the other side of the massive arrangement.

The parade of weekend customers and visitors had been both overwhelming and sweet. Shannon had never known she was so popular. The flowers dipped, and a familiar face appeared.

Shannon grinned. "Hunter! What are you doing here?"

He handed her the flowers, a lopsided smile forming across his handsome face. "Bringing beautiful flowers to an irresistible lady."

Shannon brought the flowers under her nose and took a whiff of their sweet fragrance. "Thank you. They're lovely."

He stepped closer and lowered his voice. "I've got to be honest. I was hoping we might set a time for that dinner. I guess I'm not a very patient man, and sitting around waiting for you to call is worse than waiting for a fish to migrate."

Shannon smiled again, her heart warming at what seemed like sincere intentions. "I'm sorry about that, Hunter. I've been a bit distracted. I'm sure you've heard about all of the … excitement going on here at the show."

He glanced to the side, as if to see if anyone was listening. "I did hear that someone died. Tragic."

Shannon nodded, the same ever-present sadness she felt whenever Sunny was mentioned pressing on her heart. She pointed to the empty booth beside her. "Her name was Sunny. That was her booth." She shook her head. "Her death was quite a shock."

"I can imagine. I remember seeing her work yesterday. She was good." His intense eyes captured hers, sincerity in their depths. "Are you holding up OK?"

Shannon nodded again. "Doing as well as can be expected."

Just then, her conversation with Essie replayed in her mind. Hunter had bought lead came at the shop. *Why?*

She cleared her throat. "I don't suppose you knew her, did you?"

He raised his eyebrows. "The woman who died? No. I can't say I'm an artsy kind of guy." He tilted his head. "Is there a reason you ask?"

*Not an artsy kind of guy.* Should she ask him about the lead came now? No, she'd ask later. Here he was, being nothing but sweet, and meanwhile, she was wondering if he was guilty of murder—which was crazy, since he'd made it apparent he didn't even know the woman. She smiled and said, "No reason."

"Would you like to talk over coffee tonight? It sounds like you could use a good listener."

Shannon blinked, feeling for a moment so inexperienced in the dating department. She'd been inexperienced for the past twenty years, as she'd only "dated" one man— her husband.

She cleared her throat. "Coffee? Tonight?"

He grinned, and his expression certainly could have melted the coldest of hearts. The man had charm, and he knew how to use it. "Have I mentioned that I'm not always very patient?"

Tonight … what did she have going on? Her mind felt muddled from everything that had happened. Tonight she would need to pack and clear the gym floor of her merchandise. "I wish I could, but I'm afraid I have too much to do. Perhaps another time?"

His expression fell, but only for a moment, before that same hopeful look appeared in his eyes. "Of course, you're busy with the show. How about tomorrow?"

He was persistent. Shannon would give him that. What was tomorrow? Sunday, she remembered. She had a lot to catch up on at the shop, but ...

"I'm going to church in the morning," she said. "Why don't you come with me, and then we'll grab lunch afterward?"

His grin widened. "That sounds like a plan I can live with." Noise behind him made him turn. A chattering group of women was headed straight for Shannon's booth, reminding her of the crowds on Black Friday as they raced toward a great deal.

Hunter looked back at her and took a step away. "It looks like I need to let you go. I'll see you in the morning."

Shannon found herself smiling. "See you then."

Hunter was handsome and intriguing, and he was showing a definite interest in her. She looked at her beautiful bouquet. When was the last time a man had given her flowers?

Probably not since John. It felt good to be appreciated and sought after. She'd been working so hard lately, trying to get the business off the ground and see to it that her kids were settled in at their new college. There was nothing wrong with taking time for herself.

She never wanted to become so absorbed with her business that she missed out on the other opportunities in life. She didn't want to get stuck in a rut. Each day beckoned new adventures and new opportunities to explore.

"He's a charmer," Joyce whispered. "And handsome. I like him."

"But why does the possibility of dating him fill me with both excitement and dread?"

Joyce laughed. "Because that's the way the dating game is played, my friend."

The problem was, dating made Shannon feel like someone else was playing with her heart, and that wasn't something she was entirely comfortable with.

She sighed as the chattering group of women descended on her table and began fighting over her necklaces.

As soon as she had the chance, she intended to slip away. She *had* to talk to Alana. There was no time to waste.

*     *     *

A lull in customers finally came midafternoon. Melanie had come to replace Joyce as Shannon's helper. Joyce had to get a head start on her pastries for a luncheon on Monday morning, but she didn't leave without giving an encouraging smile to Shannon—one that clearly conveyed that she was happy to see things falling into place for her friend.

With Melanie there to man the booth, Shannon slipped away for a moment, trying to look casual as she approached Alana's booth. The area was packed with too much product. It was hard to know what to look at between the numerous suncatchers, decorative boxes, night-lights, lampshades, and magnets.

"You have a good eye for color," Shannon said, picking up a night-light with a stained glass shade atop it. A beautiful flower pattern popped in bright colors on the creation, which would make a cheerful addition to any room.

Alana's lips were pulled together tightly as she sat in the chair, her arms folded across her chest. The body language wasn't especially inviting, and Shannon wondered if she was always like this or if she was simply grieving over Sunny.

The woman nodded, her expression softening slightly. "I appreciate the kind words. You're the jewelry lady. I looked at your work the other day, but you weren't at the booth. You have some very nice pieces."

"Thank you." Shannon put the night-light down and turned all of her attention on Alana. She studied the woman for a moment, noting how her face was angular and wrinkle-free. "How's the show going for you so far?"

Alana's eyes were dull as she shook her head. "I can't get over what happened."

"Did you know Sunny?"

"I did. She was like a mentor to me, even though it was I who taught her a lot of technique initially. It was a classic case of the student surpassing the teacher, I suppose." She offered another sad smile.

Shannon's heart softened. She hadn't realized that the two women had known each other so well. "That has to make you feel good, to see someone flourish who you helped get started."

Alana's arms pulled tighter across her chest. "She was wonderfully talented. Puts me to shame."

"Nonsense. Your work is very nice." Shannon spread her hand over several of the pieces. Alana's work was sure to add charm to any home. Sunny's work, however … well, it added class and breathtaking artistry.

"*Nice*? Nice doesn't equate to successful. It equates to mid-level craft shows." Alana smiled, though it didn't quite reach her eyes. "But I'm OK with that. I don't depend on this for my income. My husband passed away ten years ago and left me with a nice life insurance plan that keeps me taken care of. I do this mostly for fun."

Shannon nodded. "To be honest, I was a little surprised to learn that they let two stained glass artists into the show." She chose her words carefully, trying not to make Alana uncomfortable. She might stop talking if she felt like she was being interrogated.

"I was surprised too. When I heard that Sunny had applied to be in this show, I knew I'd never stand a chance of getting in. Imagine my surprise when they called me this week. They told me that someone else had dropped out and asked if I'd take the other person's place."

"What a lucky break. Have you done pretty well at the show, all things considered?"

"I can't complain. I'm alive, aren't I?" Alana frowned and looked off in the distance again.

Shannon studied the woman. Either she was a great actress, or she was truly grieving. "You said you knew Sunny outside of this art show. Do you think there's a chance she didn't use protective wear when she worked?"

Alana scoffed. "That's ridiculous. Of course she wore protective wear. That's rule number one when soldering, and Sunny was no dummy." The woman paused to regard Shannon a moment. "Why do you ask?"

Shannon shrugged, trying to be nonchalant. "I've heard rumors of her death being caused by poisoning—lead poisoning, to be exact."

"That's the most ridiculous thing I've ever heard! If someone wanted to poison Sunny, there are much more effective methods than lead." Alana shook her head. "No, she must have died of some unseen natural cause. A heart attack, maybe? Who knows? Either way, it's tragic."

"Out of curiosity, do you know anyone who might have wanted to hurt her?"

Alana raised an eyebrow, curiosity filling her gaze. "You may want to talk to her roommate, Erica Winters. She'd know better than I would. She was wandering around here yesterday, helping out with the show, but I haven't seen her yet today. Sunny and I got together once a week so we could catch up, but we didn't discuss anything too personal, including who our enemies were."

"How about here at the show?" Shannon asked. "Is there anyone she didn't get along with, or maybe someone she made an off-handed comment about?"

Alana paused, but only for a moment. "Talk to James Knight."

"Who's he?"

The dullness left her eyes and was replaced by a curious spark. She pointed across the room. "He's the woodcarver."

Shannon's gaze followed the pointed finger, and it landed on the same man whom she'd seen in a heated discussion the day before with the show's organizer, Mark Arnold. "Why should I talk to him?"

"The man rubs me the wrong way. I don't know ... there's something about him. I caught him staring at Sunny a lot, like he was obsessed with her or something. Plus, I saw him slipping her notes a couple of times. No doubt he'd written something creepy in them."

*Notes?* Alana had Shannon's full attention now.

"Did you ever ask Sunny about it?"

Alana shook her head. "No. Sunny didn't like to talk about her personal life too much. She preferred to immerse herself in her work, sometimes to the extent of ignoring everything else, at least for certain periods of time. Then she'd resurface for air and be social again."

That seemed to fit what Shannon had heard about Sunny from a couple of other people. A clearer picture of who Sunny was began to form in her mind.

"Thank you, Alana. I will take your advice and speak with James Knight."

*       *       *

Melanie stared across the floor at James. "He's a big bear of a man. Seems more like the type to club someone over the head than to poison them."

Shannon followed her gaze and shrugged. "He's all I've got. I'm going to talk to him."

"Do you want me to go with you?"

Shannon glanced around. "You stay here and man the booth. I'll be careful and tread lightly. I promise."

Shannon slipped over to the woodcarver's booth. It just so happened that no customers were there when she approached. She got a good look at the man. He had a neatly trimmed dark beard flecked with gray, a stocky build—and unwelcoming eyes.

*Is it my imagination, or is he glaring at me?*

Shannon shook it off. No, it was likely her imagination

working overtime. She was beginning to sound like fellow Purl, Betty Russo. Her friend always had her nose in a Jane Austen novel, and as a result, she had a very active imagination.

Shannon picked up a wall hanging made to look like the inside of an aquarium. The man's work was as detailed as it came, and it had the price tags to match. The piece Shannon held had been crafted with a scroll saw, and the intricacy of the cuts showed that James had a tremendous amount of patience. Was he patient enough to wait for Sunny to die a slow death from being poisoned over a long period of time?

"It's about time you made your way over here," James muttered at her. He brushed a speck of sawdust off his flannel shirt and stepped closer.

"Excuse me?"

He scowled at her before letting his gaze flick through the crowds. "I've been watching you question people, acting like you're the detective assigned to the case or something. I know the truth. You're just nosy."

"I beg your pardon?" Indignation rushed through Shannon. "Before you go hurling accusations, you should know I'm merely trying to get answers."

"To satisfy your curiosity?"

Shannon's hands went to her hips. "Because I'm *concerned.* Everyone deserves justice."

He leaned in closer. "You shouldn't go nosing around in places where you don't belong."

"Is that a threat?" Her Scottish accent became more pronounced as anger began to rise in her.

The man stared at her, his eyes cold and calculating for a moment, but then he visibly softened. His shoulders slumped as he sighed and stepped back. "No, it's not a threat. I've had a rough morning. Please forgive me."

"Are you upset because you're a suspect?" As the words tumbled out, she questioned the wisdom of raising the man's hackles again. "I mean—"

"A suspect?" James blinked. "*I'm* a suspect? Why in the world would *I* be a suspect?" Although the anger was gone from his voice, the man still had an edge to him.

"You tell me."

James ran a hand over his beard, his fingers tightening with tension. "Sure, Sunny and I had our share of fights and disagreements, but I would *never* hurt her."

"What did you fight about?"

He shrugged before releasing a drawn-out sigh. "It's like this. In terms of these shows, Sunny and I were the headliners. We brought in the most business. At times, things could get tense between us, especially if one person got choice placement."

"Choice placement?"

His eyes widened as if the answer should be obvious and need no explanation. "You know, more visibility—or a bigger spot in the paper. I did win a world carving competition. My work has been featured in the industry's biggest magazines, and even *Smithsonian* has talked to me about a feature there. I should be in museums and galleries."

"Then why are you here?"

"Mark Arnold always convinces me to come out for his shows. Really, I make four times as much on one commissioned piece as I do in an entire day selling Christmas ornaments and wall hangings here."

"Was it the same for Sunny?" Shannon asked. "Did Mark convince her to come?"

He shrugged. "I can't speak for Sunny. I really have no idea, but I would imagine that was the case. Otherwise, why would an artist of her caliber be here? Most of these shows are for people with hobbies. Sunny and I, we have—*had*—careers."

"Did your arguments ever go beyond issues related to booth placement?"

His eyes narrowed. "What are you implying?"

"I was just wondering how deep your dislike of each other went."

"I didn't dislike Sunny. It's just hard when there are two royals vying for the same throne, if you get my drift."

*Had the king killed the queen?*

James continued, "But I would never, *ever* hurt someone. Especially not Sunny. I knew better than to let business affect my friendships. You know?"

Based on the gleam in his eyes, Shannon found that hard to understand. Very hard to understand. She didn't quite buy his explanation for being at the show, either. He didn't strike her as a people person. Not like Sunny had been. Shannon could understand why someone like Sunny would want to leave her studio to be around fans of her work. But someone with James Knight's prickly personality? She wasn't so sure.

Shannon offered a slight smile and nodded. "I understand perfectly well."

*This man has a secret. What's he hiding?*

# 7

Shannon gunned the engine as her old truck struggled to climb the mountain road. Known as "Old Blue," the bright blue 1955 Ford pickup had once belonged to her grandfather. Even though it stalled and sputtered quite regularly, her grandmother had been unable to part with it after his death, feeling some kind of unseen connection to it. Shannon loved it for the history it held—not for its unpredictable temperament.

Her watch read 7:45, and she knew it was late to be heading out. But when she'd given Sunny's roommate, Erica Winters, a call, Erica had insisted that Shannon come by right away.

As she drove, Shannon mentally reviewed everything she'd learned. Unfortunately, nothing came close to making sense. Someone was leaving her notes, practically begging her to get involved in the case. How could she ignore that person's pleas?

As a light drizzle began to fall, Shannon flipped on her windshield wipers and listened as they scraped against the glass. The screeching sound sent a chill up her spine. Sunny's death had her wound tighter than a ball of yarn. There could be a killer on the loose in Apple Grove. She'd already experienced enough reasons not to sleep at night since she'd moved to town. She couldn't stand the thought of her community being wrapped up in the whims of a killer again.

*Maybe Erica will provide some answers.*

Shannon turned off the main road and onto a narrow lane that led her farther up the mountain. As she neared the top, the woods cleared, and a subdivision appeared, nestled on the hillside. Shannon checked the address once more before pulling into the driveway. The warm glow of a porch light spilled onto the lawn, welcoming her. She climbed from the truck and stepped onto the porch of the modern Cape Cod house. The front door boasted a beautiful stained glass window at the top. The house still maintained a cozy look, but the expansive porch and massive square footage of the structure proved it was no bungalow. Sunny must have been making serious cash with her work.

The house looked too new to have been painted with a lead-based paint. Shannon couldn't remember for sure, but she thought people had stopped using that kind of paint inside their homes in the late seventies.

Before she could knock on the door, a petite woman pulled it open. The woman held a tissue in her hand, and her face was blotchy. She had dark hair that was pulled back into a sloppy ponytail, and she wore an oversized sweatshirt like it was a blanket.

"You must be Shannon." The woman's voice sounded brittle and frail, which matched her slight frame. "I'm Erica. Come on in."

"I'm so sorry for your loss," Shannon said as she stepped inside. She wiped her feet on a rug before stepping onto the dark walnut floors. "I know how hard it is to lose someone you love."

"Thank you," Erica whispered, shutting the door against the damp cold.

Shannon's eyes widened in amazement when she saw the stained glass work displayed within the house. Nearly every window was adorned with a stained glass creation. Outside in the dark, it had been hard to see and appreciate just how detailed and plentiful the pieces were. They were even more impressive than the work Shannon had seen displayed at the show.

Erica followed her gaze. "Beautiful, aren't they?"

Shannon nodded. "They really are."

"Sunny always said, 'What fun is it if you sell all of your favorite pieces to other people and never enjoy any of your work yourself?'"

"Smart woman." Shannon touched the butterfly necklace at her throat. Another way that she could relate to Sunny—she'd saved her favorite piece for herself also. Aside from the heirloom locket she'd inherited from her grandmother, the butterfly necklace was her favorite piece of jewelry.

Erica led her into the kitchen. "This damp air chills me to the bone," she said. "Can I make you coffee or hot tea?"

"Tea would be lovely." Shannon sat at a small table nestled in the corner of the industrial-style kitchen filled with top-of-the-line stainless steel appliances. "How long were you and Sunny roommates?"

"We've been roommates off and on since college. Isn't that crazy?" Erica put a kettle on the stove and pulled two mugs from the cabinet. "I moved away for awhile and got a job in California. I got married and then divorced. I needed somewhere to stay, and Sunny offered me her place. She said she hated living alone, and that she had plenty of room."

"When did you move back here?"

"It's been two years now. Sunny and I had a great time together. We were best friends. We knew when we needed to give each other space, when the other needed to talk, and when we needed someone to be goofy with. We had the kind of great friendship that's hard to come by."

"Sounds like it." Shannon and her friend Coleen in Scotland had a similar relationship. Shannon still missed having her friend nearby. In Scotland, they'd lived on the same street. Now a face-to-face visit meant fourteen hours in an airplane for one or the other of them.

The kettle whistled, and Erica went to the stove and poured the steaming water into the waiting mugs. After asking what Shannon took in her tea, Erica added milk and sugar before setting a cup in front of her.

Shannon wrapped her hands around the mug, letting its warmth sooth her. "If you don't mind me asking, what was Sunny like this past week? Did she say or do anything unusual?"

"You sound like the police chief." Erica took a sip of her tea before hooking a stray piece of hair behind her ear. "He stopped by this morning and looked around. I gave him permission to, of course. Why wouldn't I?" She stared at her fingernails, which appeared to be chewed to the quick. "Sunny had mentioned that she wasn't feeling well last week. She thought that maybe she was tired from working too much."

"Had she been working a lot?"

Erica nodded. "She's had several pieces commissioned recently, so she was working around the clock to get them done by their deadlines. I told her she should cancel doing the show this weekend, but she wouldn't hear of it. She said it was good for her to get out of the studio and interact with people."

"That's understandable. An artist's life is one of isolation sometimes. There are moments when you need to immerse yourself into people in order to gain new perspective and ideas."

"You must be an artist yourself." Erica said, her voice cracking with each word. The woman was obviously dealing with an overwhelming amount of grief.

"I design jewelry, so I suppose I am."

"I'm the opposite of an artist. I'm an accountant."

Shannon smiled before sipping her drink again. "An admirable career."

Erica heaved in a breath, and Shannon could see the tears trying to escape. "I still can't believe she's gone."

Shannon hesitated, fidgeting with her cup. Finally, she asked, "Do you have any idea who would want to hurt her?"

"No." Erica dabbed her eyes with a wadded-up tissue. "I mean, Sunny was so easy to get along with."

"You mentioned she'd been working around the clock recently. Did that adversely affect her relationships with anyone that you're aware of?"

Erica nodded. "Her business has never been better, but her personal life was suffering."

Shannon paused mid-sip, her gut telling her she was onto something. Finally. "What do you mean?"

Erica waved her hand in the air. "Oh, it's probably nothing. It's just that she had to work a lot. It didn't leave a lot of time for other things. Her boyfriend broke up with her not too long ago because he didn't feel like he was a priority."

Shannon perked. "She had a boyfriend?"

"*Had* is the key word."

"What's his name?"

Erica shrugged and tapped her finger against her mug. "I wish I could tell you. Sunny was secretive about him—never brought him here. She was always very hush-hush about the guy. But he broke her heart when he called it quits. I think she really wanted it to work out. She just needed a little more time to finish her pieces."

"But she took time to go to the arts and crafts show," Shannon mused. "She says no to a relationship but yes to an art show?"

"*After* they broke up." Erica paused. "She said those shows reminded her of her roots."

Shannon had a feeling there was more to it. "It's a lot of work to take on simply to be reminded of your roots—right? Especially if one had pressing deadlines for other projects."

Erica shook her head. "I don't know. She didn't do any shows for a couple of years, but after they broke up, she started going again. Maybe she realized she needed to make changes in her life."

"Did she tell you anything else about him? What he did for a living? Where he lived?"

"I don't know much. My impression is that he probably lives within driving distance because they would meet on weekends sometimes. Or maybe they met halfway?" Erica shook her head again. "I'm not sure."

"Career?"

"I think he owned his own business. Based on some of the things she said, I got the feeling that he had money. He bought her a few pieces of expensive jewelry once. I still can't believe that I never met him. The whole situation was kind of weird."

Shannon nodded. She had to find out the identity of the mystery boyfriend. The question was, how?

*       *       *

As Shannon pulled onto the road leading to her home, she realized her head was pounding. She'd talked to Erica for two hours and three cups of tea. She'd tried her best to comfort the woman, who was clearly still mourning the loss of a dear friend. Shannon hadn't learned any more information about Sunny or her death after the mysterious boyfriend had been mentioned, although Erica *had* mentioned another friend of Sunny's named Lydia. The woman owned an art gallery in a town north of Apple Grove, and Shannon planned on paying her a visit in the very near future.

Now, it was almost ten o'clock, and her long day caught up with her. The craft show had been draining, as had packing up everything when it was all done. All of her jewelry was stashed in Melanie's car, and she planned to retrieve it in the morning. She loved her old truck, but with the back being uncovered, she couldn't easily haul her things around for fear of them being ruined.

Shannon's headache throbbed harder as her headlights illuminated the dark road ahead of her, the intensifying rain making it more and more difficult to see. There were still too many big missing pieces of the puzzle surrounding Sunny's death to make sense out of the mess.

Who was the boyfriend? Why hadn't Sunny shared his name with her best friend?

Was this really a case of murder … or just a tragic accident caused by improper use of her equipment and chemicals?

With each question, the ache in Shannon's head pounded harder. She rubbed her temples with one hand, trying to ease the pain.

Maybe she *should* step back and let the authorities handle all of it. She had enough to handle on her own, and she wasn't exactly qualified to investigate a suspicious death, unless one counted the previous mysteries she'd solved. But she did have a knack for finding answers.

*Someone* seemed to think she could get to the bottom of it. That had to be why he or she had left the notes for her. The person obviously realized she had an insatiable curiosity, also, and wouldn't easily rest until she knew the truth.

She pulled into the long driveway leading to her home, which was situated quite a way from the road. She drove up the hill to the circle drive and cut the engine. Part of the Paisley mansion remained spotlighted by her headlights. Its tan stucco exterior and terra-cotta tile roof came alive with angular shadows. A wide stone staircase led to the grand entrance of the house, and gardens flanking either side gave the house a majestic feeling.

The building itself was huge and lovely, more than she could have ever imagined. But living in it alone with her housekeeper wasn't exactly her ideal—not that she didn't adore Deborah. *What would it be like to live here with someone I loved? To get married again? To have someone to help carry life's burdens?*

Hunter Banks's image flickered through her mind. Could they have a future together? Her gut told her it was a ridiculous thought—she barely knew the man. But she needed to give people a chance. Church and lunch together would answer some questions, she hoped.

Unwelcome thoughts of Michael demanded her attention. She shook her head as her hand rested on the door handle of the truck. Michael wasn't interested. He might not ever be interested, so she had to get the idea out of her head and her heart. There were other fish in the sea, so to speak.

She climbed out of the truck to find that the rain had died down to a light mist. The grass was wet at her feet as she slogged to the front door. Thankfully, Deborah had left the front light on. It helped to ward away some of the chill she felt from thinking far too often about murder.

She stepped onto the porch and paused, staring at the piece of paper stuck between the storm door and the front door.

Her back muscles tensed as she turned. She surveyed the area around her. She saw no one. Still, the uneasy feeling lingered.

*Is someone hiding in the trees ... watching me?*

She carefully slid the paper out and opened it. Her blood went ice cold as the words stared back at her: "Careful, or you might be the next victim."

# 8

Shannon enjoyed a wonderful morning at church. The worship service was uplifting and the sermon inspiring, but being with Hunter added another layer of excitement. He was charming and gracious. He never failed to open the door for her or pull out her chair or retrieve her hymnal when she accidentally dropped it.

She'd seen Michael across the room, and he'd waved from his pew on the other side of the church. But he didn't stick around after the service to say hello.

"Any preference for lunch?" Hunter asked, grinning, with his hands stuffed into his pockets in a casual manner. They stood in the narthex of the church while people milled around them, chatting and talking about plans for the day.

"I was wondering how you might feel about taking a trip to Cannon Beach," Shannon said. "It's a little coastal town about an hour's drive from here. It sits on the edge of Ecola State Park. I've heard lots of good things about the place but haven't had the opportunity to visit."

"Cannon Beach?" Hunter thought for a moment. "Isn't that where Haystack Rock is?"

She nodded. "It is, but that's not why I want to go there. It's got an art gallery I'd like to visit. I'm sure we can find somewhere to eat while we're in town."

"Your wish is my command." Hunter offered an exaggerated bow, which brought a smile to Shannon's face.

They climbed into his truck. It was a newer vehicle that was much more reliable than Old Blue, but it didn't have nearly as much personality. The engine purred after he turned the key, and she gave him directions on which way to go.

Erica had mentioned that Sunny's work was displayed at a gallery in Cannon Beach, and that the owner had been a good friend. Shannon figured it couldn't hurt to take a drive there and see if she could find any new information.

She also needed to ask Hunter about the lead came he'd purchased, but dread pooled in her stomach at the thought. Certainly he had a logical explanation. It wasn't like he knew Sunny, so there was no reason to suspect he had a connection with her death. But Shannon had learned that everyone had secrets, some of them darker than others—things they'd rather not have brought to light. Was Hunter hiding something also?

He glanced her way as they cruised down the road, and then casually draped his arm on the console between the seats. "What's so special about this art gallery?"

"I want to talk to the woman who runs it. No big deal, really, but Sunday is the best day for me to make trips like this."

"Does this have anything to do with that artist who died?"

"It does, actually." Heaviness pressed on Shannon as she said the words aloud. "I don't know why I can't let Sunny's death go, but I can't. I *know* she was murdered, and I can't stand the thought of her killer walking free."

"Aren't the police investigating?"

Shannon nodded. "They are, but not nearly fast enough for my taste."

"It hasn't even been 48 hours."

Shannon glanced sideways at him, a slight furrow between her brows.

"I'm merely pointing out a fact." He flashed a charming grin. "You're bold, and you don't let things stop you when you have a goal. I like that."

"Thanks. Not everyone feels the same way," Shannon said, Chief Grayson coming to mind.

"I'm sure the people you've helped do. That must give you some satisfaction."

Shannon couldn't deny his words. And it was refreshing to hear someone say they understood her reason for doing the things she did. Michael always seemed completely at odds with her nosiness.

Shannon took a deep breath. *Now is as good a time as ever to ask Hunter about the lead came.* She tried to keep her voice light as she said, "Essie mentioned that you were in the shop last week."

Hunter nodded, raising a hand in mock surrender while the other remained safely on the steering wheel. "You caught me. I was hoping to run into you, but you were on an errand."

"Did you find anything while you were there?" She tried to sound casual, refusing to let her emotions be sidetracked by his admission.

"As a matter of fact, I did. I found just what I needed to fix some of my equipment. Your store saved the day."

She cut her gaze sharply toward him as she tried to make sense of his words. "What equipment?"

"My scuba gear." He pointed his thumb toward the back

of his truck where something jostled with each turn. "I've learned to repair it myself. I use lead came to solder certain parts of the equipment."

Shannon nearly laughed out loud. He *did* have a reasonable explanation! Who would have thought? Her relief must have shown on her face.

"You didn't think …?" He scrunched his eyebrows together.

Shannon shook her head. "The timing was just uncanny."

"I suppose I could agree with that."

She shifted in her seat, eager to change the subject. "So how's your project going?" Hunter had come to town to work as a marine biologist, researching the dietary habits of the black rockfish or something of the sort. He'd mentioned it to her when they'd first met.

"It's going quite well," he said. "I've grown to love this area of Oregon. It's beautiful."

"Certainly you miss your home a little. California—right?"

"That's right. And yes, I do miss it a tiny bit." He grinned at her. "But I've found some nice distractions here."

Shannon chuckled. "You do have a way with words."

His grin widened. "I try."

They pulled onto the main street that ran through the picturesque downtown of Cannon Beach, and the art gallery—The Glass House—immediately came into view. It was located on a corner with a lovely wooden sign hanging from the front. Shannon pointed out the building. "Do you mind if we stop there first?"

"Not in the least." Hunter pulled into a parking space in front of the gallery, cut the engine, and ran around to open the door for Shannon.

As soon as she stepped out of the truck, the salty air from the ocean filled her senses. She'd always loved that smell, ever since she was a child living on the Scotland coast. Something about the scent brought a comfort that never got old.

Hunter stopped beside her. "Now *that* is beautiful."

She opened her eyes, realizing that she'd paused and lost herself in the moment. She stared at the water beyond them. "It sure is."

"I was talking about you."

She glanced over and saw him staring at her. She found herself blushing, something she hadn't done for a long time. She laughed it off, raising her finger and shaking it at him. "You ..."

He was good—too good.

"What?" He shrugged in mock innocence as they began walking toward the gallery.

At a loss for words, she could only shake her head at him. He could make her blush—and she couldn't say that about most people.

"That's a *good* shake of the head, right?" He pulled the door open, a lopsided grin on his face.

She pulled her lips together a moment before saying, "We'll see."

A lemon-clean scent met them when they stepped inside the gallery. Shannon's attention was immediately drawn to the beautiful works of art around them. This wasn't just any art gallery. It was a place that sold only the best of the best, and Sunny's work was among it—and rightfully so.

"Welcome to The Glass House." A woman in her mid-forties

with tight red curls piled on top of her head emerged from a back room. She looked prim and professional in a navy blue pantsuit, complete with a strand of pearls around her neck. "Let me know if I can help you with anything."

"Actually, you *can* help me with something," Shannon said as the woman started to step away.

The woman put her hands together, her face drawn into tight lines. "OK." She extended her hand. "I'm Lydia, by the way."

Shannon shook her hand. "I'm Shannon McClain, and this is Hunter Banks. I own the Paisley Craft Market & Artist Lofts in Apple Grove."

Her face softened. "Apple Grove? Such a fabulous little town. What brings you here, if you don't mind me asking?"

Shannon pointed to one of the colorful panes hanging near one of the shop's massive windows. "Sunny Davis."

Lydia's lips pulled downward. "What a tremendous loss to the art world. Sunny was an amazing artist. Who knows what masterpiece she would have created next?"

"You knew her well?"

Lydia nodded, absently rubbing her pearl necklace. "I was the first gallery to sell her work. I discovered her when she had a booth at a craft show in Portland, and I knew she had talent. Nearly everything I've ever had of Sunny's has sold. Some customers have even fought over her work. She was very popular."

"People fought over her work, you say?" Shannon mulled the thought. It was a possibility she hadn't seriously considered— that maybe it was one of Sunny's admirers who was guilty of murder.

"Yes. We had two women in here one time who were vying for one of her pieces, and I thought they were going to get into a fistfight. One left to get money to buy a wall hanging. While she did that, another woman came in, and they were both at the register trying to buy the same item at the same time. What a mess!" Lydia threw her hands in the air as if even remembering the moment frustrated her.

Shannon stored the information in the back of her mind.

Lydia looked back at the stained glass creations behind her and sighed. "Of course, all of Sunny's work will now probably rise in value. That generally happens when an artist dies."

Shannon's back stiffened. That would certainly give someone a motive for murder—including gallery owners like Lydia. She'd make more money, at least temporarily, on every piece of Sunny's work she sold. "Lydia, I understand that you and Sunny were friends. Did she ever mention anything about a boyfriend to you?"

Lydia began wiping the countertop by the register with a microfiber cloth even though the dark wood already looked polished and shiny.

*She's either a neat freak, or she's nervous.*

"A boyfriend?" Lydia repeated. "No. Sunny was married to her work. She didn't have time for that. She barely had time for her roommate."

Shannon leaned her hip against the counter. "Do you know her roommate, Erica?"

"Sure. Erica followed Sunny around everywhere. She was like a lost puppy, and Sunny was too nice to turn her away."

"That's interesting," Shannon said. "I got the impression they were good friends." Had Erica stretched the truth?

"They were. Until Erica got divorced. Then she became what I like to call 'needy.' I don't know where the poor girl will go now. She lost her job a couple of months ago, you know. Sunny didn't have the heart to kick her out."

Erica hadn't mentioned losing her job. She'd said she was an accountant. Something wasn't adding up. "Why did Sunny want to kick her out?"

"For being high maintenance? For not giving her any personal space?" Lydia shrugged. "I'm not sure."

Shannon nodded, trying to come to terms with the new information. "I had no idea things were strained between them."

"Sunny usually didn't talk too much about personal stuff like that, but she came here to drop off merchandise one day when she was feeling particularly frustrated, I think. She told me how suffocated she was feeling. I felt bad for Sunny. She was stuck between the proverbial rock and hard place."

"Did you ever hear an update? Did they resolve anything?"

Lydia shook her head. "I wouldn't know. Sunny told me about that the last time she was in here, and that was the last time we spoke." She cast a curious glance at Shannon. "You're awfully interested in her."

Shannon decided it was time to get to the heart of the matter. "I'm interested in finding out who killed her. Do you have any idea who might've wanted Sunny dead?"

Lydia paused from her polishing. "I heard a rumor that she was poisoned. I still can't believe it. But, to answer your question, no. I can't imagine anyone wanting to hurt her. If you put a gun to my head and made me choose someone, I'd say it was Mark Arnold."

"His name seems to come up a lot. Why would you think of him?"

Lydia shrugged and hauled in a deep breath. "Just a gut feeling. I can't prove anything. I think he was the mastermind behind some dirty tactics used to get people like James Knight and Sunny to his shows. Those shows have gone downhill in recent years, and he was desperate for money. Desperation can lead people to do funny things."

Shannon couldn't agree more.

*    *    *

Shannon and Hunter stepped out of the shop, and before Shannon could rehash any of the conversation with Hunter, her cellphone rang. She paused on the sidewalk and pulled her phone from her purse. Joyce had gifted her with a jeweled cellphone cover that made the device easy to spot in the depths of her oversized bag.

Shannon didn't recognize the number. "Hello?"

"Shannon? It's Alana Golden. I'm not sure if you remember me."

Shannon's eyebrows shot toward the sky. "Of course I do. We met at the show."

"That's right. Listen, I remembered something about Sunny that I thought you'd like to know. You seemed interested in figuring out what happened to her when we spoke, and I'm so glad." Alana paused, and Shannon thought she heard a sniff. "Someone needs to find out what happened to her. Do you have time to get together and talk?"

Shannon's pulse raced with excitement. "I'd love to. When are you thinking?"

"How about tomorrow afternoon?"

"That works. Where?"

"Would you mind driving out to my place? I've got students coming later in the day, so I won't have much time for travel."

"That would be fine. Where do you live exactly?"

Shannon jotted the address on a scrap of paper, hit END, and then turned to Hunter, who stood waiting patiently on the sidewalk beside her. "Sorry about that."

"No need to apologize. You're quite the detective." He placed his hand on her back as they began to stroll along the sidewalk.

She pulled her coat closer, chilled by the brisk autumn air. "I don't know about that. I like finding answers. And I enjoy talking to people in the process. I never realized solving mysteries would be something I was good at, but I have had some success in the past."

"What do you think? Give up jewelry making and the craft store, and open your own P.I. agency?" Hunter's face almost looked comical as he raised an eyebrow and tilted his head.

Shannon chuckled at the idea. "Oh, no. I'm not interested in that. Besides, once I officially declared myself a professional investigator, no one would want to speak with me. Part of the reason people talk to me is because I'm an everyday, ordinary person."

"With a fabulous accent."

Shannon laughed. "You like the accent, do you?"

"It's charming."

"As are you."

They continued their leisurely stroll down the sidewalk, and Shannon soaked in the shops around her. The place reminded her of some of the small towns in Scotland that she used to visit. Communities like this had their lure for a reason.

Hunter cleared his throat and shoved his hands into the pockets of his wool jacket. "It sounds like the web has become more tangled. Do you have any solid suspects?"

"Solid? No. But there are definitely people with means, motive, and opportunity. The question is, which one has all three?"

"That is the question, Sherlock. I'm sure you'll have the answers in no time." He paused in front of a café with ruffled curtains and cheerful flowers in the boxes on the windows. "This place looks good. What do you say?"

Her stomach grumbled in response. "I say let's find a table."

They walked inside the quaint restaurant that had tables and chairs scattered haphazardly throughout the small space. Patrons chattered as their silverware clamored against their plates and bowls. The scent of French fries mixed with that of cinnamon, creating a surprisingly pleasant combination.

A waitress seated them by the window and placed two menus before them. Shannon decided on the clam chowder, and Hunter ordered a burger and fries. With the waitress gone, they settled back to chat.

Shannon took a sip of her water and studied Hunter for a moment. "Does it offend you as a marine biologist that I'm eating sea creatures?"

He laughed, his green eyes sparkling. "Not at all. I was in the mood for something hearty today, if you know what I mean. Otherwise I might be eating sea creatures myself. They're awfully tasty."

She crossed her arms and leaned back in her wooden chair. "How long do you plan on staying in Apple Grove?"

Hunter shrugged. "I'm not sure yet. As long as it takes to get this project done."

"Did you always want to be a marine biologist?" She asked, thinking that crossing her arms might look too stand-offish. She grabbed her water and played with her straw instead, trying remember how to properly act on a date.

"Pretty much. My mom always called me a fish because I wouldn't stay out of the water. I set up an aquarium for myself when I was six, and I was fascinated with the little underwater world it brought into my life. The love never died, so it was only natural that I studied marine biology. I love it enough that I teach it as well. I'm an adjunct professor in marine biology at Lawson College in California." He leaned closer. "How about you? How'd you get started in the arts and crafts business?"

"I've always loved creating things. When my twins were little, I started making jewelry and knitting—just for fun, really. But then people started showing an interest in my work. I realized that I actually had some talent and started an online business."

"You have a lot of talent." His gaze was focused completely on her as he stared at her from across the table.

She smiled, trying to ward away niggling feelings of giddiness. "Thank you."

"What brought you here all the way from Scotland?"

"I came to Oregon after I found out that a grandmother I never knew had died and left me her estate. It's a long story—believe me. And it sounds like something that would only happen in a movie, only it really did happen to me."

He raised his eyebrows. "Wow. I'd like to hear about it sometime."

"It's been a real blessing. Everyone in town has been so welcoming, and I've made some very good friends in Apple Grove."

He tilted his head. "You said 'estate.' I've been to your house a couple of times. Is there more to it than that?"

Shannon nodded. "Yes, and that's an understatement. The property and house that were left to me are astounding. More than I could have ever dreamed. I'll have to give you a tour of the property one day."

His smile was her reward. "I'd like that."

Their food came, and they ate for several minutes in comfortable silence. Finally, Shannon spoke. "My late husband was a geologist."

"Was he?" Hunter stared at her a moment. "If you don't mind me asking, what happened?"

"Car accident. It was terrible."

Hunter's hand covered hers, and warmth spread through her. "I'm sorry, Shannon. I can't imagine how hard that must have been."

"Thanks." She cleared her throat, realizing the conversation had become much more serious than she'd intended. "How about you? Ever been married?"

He shook his head. "Came close once."

"Fear of commitment?" she teased.

A gleam shone in his eyes. "Not in the least. I've just been looking for the right person."

She raised her brows, picking up on his implications all too well. "I see."

They finished their lunch, talking about everything from the best places to visit while in town to their dream vacations. The conversation was a nice change in topic from murder, and Hunter was a perfect gentlemen.

But despite the lighthearted feel of the moment, Shannon couldn't shake the unease that had plagued her since Sunny died. She couldn't simply forget the fact that there was still a murderer on the loose—and much work to be done to catch him ... or her.

# 9

Shannon slipped into her office at the Paisley Craft Market to catch up on some of her paperwork when she returned from her lunch date with Hunter. Being tied up at the craft show for three days had caused her to fall behind. Essie and Melanie and the other part-timers had covered the floor for her on those days, but Shannon was the one who kept the books straight. The store closed at five on Sundays, and that gave her some time to work alone.

She'd only been in her office for an hour when she heard someone pound on the front door to the shop. Instantly, her guard went up. No one knew she was in the store. Images of the shadowy figure who'd been leaving her cryptic messages filled her mind.

She stepped out of her office and peeked around the corner.

Chief Grayson waved at her through the glass.

She blew out a sigh of relief and hurried to unlock the door.

"Hello, Shannon," Grayson said as he stepped inside. "You got a minute to talk?"

"Sure. Let's go to my office." She offered him a seat, pointing to a dainty Victorian chair. "I'd offer you coffee, but all the machines are off."

"I'm fine. Thank you." Grayson didn't take the offer of a seat.

"How'd you know I was here?" Shannon didn't want to take a defensive posture, so she continued to stand as well.

"No one else drives a truck like yours. I saw it parked out front."

"Of course." Her cheeks heated. Some detective she was. It was a fairly obvious clue. "I've been expecting you."

He raised his eyebrows. "Expecting me?"

"I figured you'd stop by and ask if anyone purchased any lead came here. We do sell it." She watched his reaction carefully and saw the telltale twitch of his lips.

"Very good, Shannon. And …?"

She leaned against her desk and crossed her arms. "We've had two people purchase the product in the past month. One was Dina Miller, who is a stained glass enthusiast. The other was Hunter Banks, who said he bought it to fix some of his scuba equipment."

The chief stared at her a moment before nodding. "It sounds like you've been thorough."

She shrugged. "I try."

"I know I've told you this before, but—"

She raised her hands in surrender. "I should let the police handle the investigation. Yes, you have mentioned that before."

"In the past, that advice has never seemed to sink in."

"I have more connections in the art world than you do, Chief."

"And I'm more highly trained in both investigating and in protecting myself in case something goes wrong."

Her hands went to her hips. "I just want answers. I'm assuming that since you came in here to ask about the lead came, this is an official murder investigation now?"

The chief pulled his lips into a tight line, and tipped his hat toward her. "Good day, Shannon. I'll be in touch."

*I'm right. This is officially a murder investigation.*

Just as Grayson breezed out the door, Melanie and Kate Ellis slipped inside. Melanie's eyes looked a little brighter than usual as she sidled up to Shannon with a big grin on her face. Her smile slipped when she looked back at the chief. She hadn't been particularly fond of the man since he'd wrongly arrested her for the murder of her ex-husband.

"What's *he* doing here?" Melanie asked.

"Asking questions. Doing his job." Shannon sighed. "Telling me not to get involved."

"Doing what he does best, I suppose. I only hope he doesn't put the wrong person behind bars again." Melanie frowned.

"It can be hard to trust the justice system sometimes, but it's what we've got to do. I'm merely trying to help them along—whether they like it or not." Shannon offered a mischievous grin.

The trio of friends took seats in Shannon's office, Melanie in a plush Victorian chair on one side of Shannon, and Kate on the other side. Kate, who was in her early thirties, owned the dog grooming and walking service, Ultimutt Grooming. She'd become a trusted friend in the time since Shannon had been in Apple Grove. She was also one of the Purls.

Melanie leaned toward Shannon. "I saw you sitting with Hunter at church, and then you two disappeared afterward. What's going on?"

"You don't waste any time, do you?" Shannon laughed. "We had lunch together. A nice, friendly lunch." She sliced her hand through the air to show the finality of her words.

Melanie stared at her, an expression of disbelief on her face. "That's it? Come on. There has to be more to tell than that."

"That's right," Kate said. "We want to live vicariously through your love life—we need something to take the place of our lackluster ones."

"Truly, that's all there is to report. Alas, there's no wedding for you to start planning." Shannon offered an apologetic smile.

"I really want to do the flowers for you whenever the big day comes," Melanie said.

"Joyce already volunteered to both make your cake and to bedazzle your dress," Kate said with a grin.

Shannon raised an eyebrow. "It sounds like you've all been talking about this at length."

"Joyce, Essie, Kate, and I ran into each other at lunch." Melanie shrugged. "We got to talking, and the topic may have come up. There's nothing we love more than a good wedding."

"Except to see a member of the Purls happy," Kate chimed in.

Shannon wrestled with indecision. Should she tell them about Rupert's unofficial offer and the potential relocation it would require? She hadn't told anyone yet for fear of upsetting the flow of her life by talking about the possibility of moving. She cleared her throat, deciding that talking about it might prove therapeutic. "I got a job offer."

"A job offer?" Melanie asked, confusion on her face. "But you already have one."

"True," Shannon said. "This one is with R & M Designs."

Kate's mouth dropped open. "They're *big*. That's awesome, Shannon."

Shannon shrugged. "I guess."

Melanie leaned closer. "You *guess*? What does that

mean? What's there to guess about? People *dream* about opportunities like that."

Shannon heaved in a deep breath. "I'm under the impression that the job would require a move."

The jovial mood in the room turned somber. Melanie shook her head as if rattled at the thought. "But people telecommute all the time. Why would it require a move?"

"I'm not really sure of the details."

Kate glanced around the shop. "What would that mean for the store? Would you sell it?"

Shannon waved her hand in the air as if the idea were absurd. "No way would I ever sell this store. It's practically like a family member, as are all of you."

Melanie's smile was nowhere to be seen. "You should do it. It's a great opportunity, and you deserve to have your work rewarded. We'll be able to say that we knew you back when ..."

Shannon shifted her weight, picking a few stray leaves from the rag rug at her feet. She needed to move on to a conversation that she was more excited to talk about—murder. "I did find out more information about Sunny today."

"Tell, tell." Melanie's eyes brightened again.

Shannon told her friends about her conversation with Lydia, who'd pointed the finger at both Mark Arnold and Erica Winters. She also told them about the realization that Sunny's work would be worth even more, now that she was dead.

Melanie raised an eyebrow. "You know where you need to look now—right?"

"Where?"

Melanie leaned closer and lowered her voice. "You need

to look into who's receiving the profits from her work upon her death. *That* would be a motive for murder."

Kate nodded. "Melanie's right. Follow the money."

Shannon leaned against the desk and nodded. That *would* be a motive for murder. But how was she going to find out who that person was?

\*       \*       \*

Before Melanie and Kate left the market, they helped Shannon unload her jewelry from the back of Melanie's car. Just seeing the pieces reminded her of the art show, which reminded Shannon of Sunny's death, which then reminded her that no one should get away with murder.

As she put the last box in her office, she got a text from Michael, asking if she wanted to go out for coffee at eight. He said he had some information to share.

*Interesting.*

Their meeting couldn't come soon enough.

She straightened her desk and killed time until finally, the clock on the wall read eight. She grabbed her coat and purse and headed outside. Punctual as always, Michael stood waiting for her on the sidewalk outside the front door as she locked up. The sight of him caused her heart rate to quicken. He was a handsome man. She couldn't deny that. But, handsome or not, they were just friends. *Just friends.*

The wind swirled around them as she stepped onto the sidewalk. Her eyes traveled upward to meet his, and a smile stretched across her face. "How are you today? I didn't have a chance to speak with you at church."

He walked slowly and leisurely down South Main Street, but his eyes held a certain heaviness that brought a measure of concern to her. "Can't complain. And you?"

"Fine. I suppose I can't complain either." No, she treasured each day she was alive and in good health.

"I thought maybe we could grab a cup of coffee at Grandma May's place. The change of scenery might be nice."

"That works for me. Grandma May serves a mean cup of coffee."

Part of his lip curled as he glanced her way. "I still can't believe you turned into a coffee drinker. I distinctly recall that you'd only drink tea when you first arrived in the States. I daresay you were almost snobbish about it," he teased.

"Coffee's growing on me." She smiled up at him, anxious to hear what he had to tell her.

They strolled past the gardens that comprised the town square of Apple Grove. The old-fashioned gas lampposts along the streets and sidewalks were lit, giving the community a warm feel despite the chilly weather. In the summertime, tourists came to the area to explore the beaches; a trolley ran from the town to the beach. In December and March, whale-watching tours did a rousing business.

Arriving at Grandma May's, a newer home-style diner in town, Michael and Shannon found a corner seat inside. They waved hello to a couple of familiar faces in the restaurant before ordering their own coffee and settling in to talk.

Shannon leaned toward Michael, rubbing her arms to ward away the cool chill that floated in every time someone opened the door. "I can't take the suspense any longer. What's going on? Why do you look so grim?"

His eyes looked heavy. In fact, even his shoulders drooped as if something were pulling them downward. "I've been contemplating whether or not to tell you this, Shannon."

She was shocked that he was going to tell her any "insider information" about the case at all. But the ominous tone of his voice caused her to tense as anticipation settled in. "You know you can trust me, Michael."

His gaze flickered to hers again. He spread his fingers over the table, almost as if bracing himself to speak. "It's about Hunter."

Her heart sank. "Hunter?"

He nodded and let out a long sigh. "Shannon, there is no Bayside Marine Research Associates."

Her anxiety turned to ice-cold shock. "What are you talking about?"

His palms turned upward, and his earnest gaze remained on her. "The company Hunter claims to work for. There's no business by that name anywhere in the U.S."

Shannon shook her head, a million thoughts racing through her mind. "Maybe it's small. Maybe it's not listed in the normal places. Maybe it's new. Who knows? There are a lot of reasons you might not be able to find a listing for it. Besides, it's not his only source of income. He's also an adjunct professor in marine biology at Lawson College in California."

Michael's expression didn't change, and he definitely didn't concede to her theory. Instead, he stared at Shannon as if waiting for her to draw the right conclusions.

But what would those right conclusions be?

"Michael?" She studied him, hoping his expression might give something away. It didn't.

He shrugged with regret. "I'm just telling you what I discovered."

"Why would Hunter fabricate a business and come here claiming to be a marine biologist under false circumstances?"

He shrugged. "That I can't tell you. There's no shortage of reasons why people might want to deceive others."

"It wouldn't make any sense to lie about that." Shannon wasn't sure why she felt the need to defend Hunter. Maybe it was because she'd felt a spark with him that she hadn't experienced in a while.

"I didn't say that it made sense. But I thought you should know."

Suddenly her coffee didn't look tempting at all. She pushed the cup away and leaned closer to Michael. "Tell me this. Why were you looking into Hunter? As a part of one of your investigations?"

Shannon thought she caught him flinch at the question, but just as quickly, Michael's unwavering expression returned. "There's something about the man that doesn't sit right with me."

Shannon blinked. Could Michael be *jealous*? Surely not. "He's a perfectly decent man, Michael. You're not making sense."

He raised his palms to the air again. "I can't explain it. It's a gut feeling."

"You think he has something to do with Sunny's death?"

He shook his head. "I didn't say that. I said my gut feeling is that he's hiding something."

If she were thinking in her right frame of mind, she would admit that Michael did have a knack for sensing the truth in people. Years of working as a detective had conditioned him to be like that. But Michael was wrong about Hunter—she was certain that he was a stand-up guy.

"I didn't mean to upset you," he said, calmly sipping his coffee.

Again, Michael's human radar detector was going full force. Shannon didn't bother to hide her emotions. "You don't want to date me," she blurted, "but you don't want anyone else to date me either. That's not fair, Michael."

Michael paled. "What? I never said I didn't want to date you. It's just ... complicated."

"I'll say." She chewed on the inside of her mouth, desperately wishing she hadn't brought up the topic.

Michael drew in a deep breath. "I'm not going to apologize for looking into Hunter. I thought you should know what I discovered. End of story."

She stared at the table, unsure of what to say and afraid to look up and let Michael see the emotions in her eyes. The last thing she wanted was for Michael to suspect that she still had strong—and complicated—feelings for him.

Finally, Michael stood. "Look, how about we call it a night? I'll walk you to your truck."

She nodded, knowing that any more attempts at a pleasant conversation would fall flat. Michael dropped some money on the table, waved at the waitress, and they stepped outside. Lately, things had been awkward between them, but at that moment, the tension between them was palpable.

Shannon paused on the sidewalk, trying to think of a way to gracefully end their conversation. She needed to let her emotions to cool off. She surveyed everything around her as she tried to find the right words.

That's when her skin prickled as something unseen heightened her senses. Her head swiveled from left to right, searching for the source of her fear.

Michael's hand covered her arm. "What is it?"

"I can't get over this feeling that I'm being watched." Yet all she saw were the cars parked along the street, a few ornamental trees, decorative lampposts, and a string of shops.

His eyes soaked in everything around him. "How long have you felt this way?"

"Since last night, when I found an unnerving note on my porch." Her heart pounded in her ears as adrenaline coursed through her.

"What kind of note?"

She was hesitant to share, especially in light of their recent conversation. But she couldn't let her stubbornness get in the way of the murder investigation.

"It warned me to be careful, or I'd be the next victim." Movement in the distance caught her eye. Her finger jutted out, pointing toward the shadow darting behind a large SUV. "There! Did you see that? Someone's hiding behind that vehicle."

# — 10 —

"Stay here!" Michael told Shannon.

No sooner had he taken his first step toward the SUV did someone jet out from behind it. The figure darted toward an alleyway between two shops in the distance. The person was dressed in black from head to toe, including the baseball cap on her head.

*Her head.*

The way she moved, her build ... Shannon was certain that the slight figure was a woman.

*A woman's behind this?*

The woman darted behind a building before Michael could reach her. She'd had too much of a head start. Even though Michael's legs were long, there was too much distance between them for Michael to close the space.

Shannon put a hand over her mouth. She wanted to run, to chase the woman also, but she knew she was too far away to help. Standing frozen, like a petrified tree, watching everything happen, made her feel helpless.

A gunshot rang out.

"Michael!" she screamed, her heart pounding. She couldn't see him anymore. He'd disappeared behind the building.

Her breathing felt labored. *I have to do something!*

Before she could question herself, she raced toward the alley where Michael had disappeared. If he'd been shot, then he needed help. She needed to call an ambulance.

Her chest squeezed with anxiety. *Please, let him be OK!* If he was hurt, then it would be all her fault. She'd pulled him into this mess.

Tears flooded her eyes, blurring her vision, and she collided with someone.

Shannon gasped, fearing it was the killer. "Och! Let go of me!" she shrieked.

"Shannon? Are you hurt?"

Her vision cleared. Michael. It was Michael. *Thank you, Lord.*

"Shannon?" He grasped her arms, worry wrinkling between his eyes.

She nodded. "I'm fine. I heard the gunshot …"

"That woman is either a terrible shot, or she was deliberately trying to miss me."

Shannon tilted her head as she tried to comprehend his meaning. It was no use. Her nerves and mind were still frazzled. "Why would she try to miss?"

"To keep me back and buy herself enough time to get away."

Shannon's head began to clear. "You thought she was a woman too? It wasn't just my imagination?"

"I'd never be able to pick her out of a lineup, but there's no doubt in my mind that person was a female."

She swallowed hard, trying to regain control of her emotions. "What happened to her?"

"She jumped into a little sedan and sped off before I could reach her."

"License plate?"

He shook his head. "It was covered in mud. I couldn't read it."

"What do you think she was doing?"

"Your guess is as good as mine. Spying on you? About to shoot you? Who knows?"

Shannon rubbed her arms, the night air suddenly feeling even chillier. "I don't like this."

His piercing blue gaze met hers. "I don't like this, either, Shannon. I'm worried for your safety."

Shannon bit her lip. For the first time since Sunny's death, she was truly afraid for herself also.

*      *      *

Michael followed Shannon home that night so he could check out her house and make sure no one with ill intentions was lurking about. Of course, he'd insisted on calling Grayson first to report what had happened. Shannon now knew her suspicions were right—someone had followed her the previous night. That same person had a gun and had fired it at Michael.

At the Paisley mansion, everything was calm. Deborah was out; she'd gone to play cards with some friends. After checking every potential entry point of the mansion and the grounds around the main house, Michael left with instructions for Shannon to call the police immediately if she noticed anything suspicious.

What had seemed like a personal vendetta against Sunny—and Sunny only—suddenly seemed like something much more dangerous, and the stakes of Shannon's involvement in the whole mystery had become much greater.

*Am I being targeted because of the investigation? Or for another reason?*

The good news, Shannon realized, was that whoever was behind it all appeared to be a woman. That knowledge narrowed her suspects considerably. Unfortunately, it didn't afford her much peace. There were still too many unanswered questions.

Those questions haunted her all night as she tossed and turned, trying to sleep—questions about the mysterious woman's identity, about Michael's claim that Hunter's business was bogus, and about his reason for investigating Hunter in the first place. Should she even venture to ask Hunter about it? Or should she trust that his reasons for being here were genuine? And did that really matter if Michael's suspicions about Hunter were true?

It was all too much.

The next morning, dark circles lined Shannon's eyes. Her already pale skin didn't do her any favors. It would be obvious to everyone that something was wrong. Even a hot shower did no good.

*Perhaps a nice hot cup of tea will help.*

Her head still feeling hazy, she put a kettle of water on the stove. Absently, she spooned tea leaves into an infuser and waited for the water to boil. Finally, the shrill whistle of the teakettle filled the room. Shannon poured the water into her cup, sat at the table, and stared outside at the sunlight that filtered through the tree limbs into the front yard.

Her cellphone interrupted the peaceful moment.

It was Rupert Murphy, the president of R & M Designs. Shannon braced herself for the conversation and the emotional upheaval that would invariably come with it. So-called success was tempting ... but at what price?

"Mrs. McClain," he said in an authoritative manner. "Have you given our conversation some thought?"

She licked her lips. "A little. I haven't had time to seriously consider it though."

Rupert sighed with impatience. "What's there to consider? I'm offering you the opportunity to design jewelry full time, Shannon. I think you've got what it takes. Of course, I'd pay to move you out to Chicago—"

"Couldn't I work from home?" That was the most pressing question in the forefront of her mind.

"We like to have all of our designers close to our company headquarters. We do a lot of collaborative work and training. Plus, I'd want you to oversee a design team, who'd be helping you with your line."

Her own line. That sounded big.

But even bigger was the knot forming in her stomach at the thought of having to move.

"Chicago?" Shannon said, recalling that he'd mentioned moving her out of the "rinky-dink" town of Apple Grove. At the time, she hadn't realized there was no room for compromise on the issue.

"It's just a place to live," he said. "You could keep your place where you live now and fly back there once a month, if you wanted. Your work would be featured in *all* of my stores, and we'd make your line a household name. You're already developing your brand—we could help you."

*Shannon McClain a household name? My brand?* She nearly snorted with amusement at the thought. She didn't, of course. "I'm flattered. I really am. But … I don't know." She took a sip of tea, praying it would calm her nerves.

"Most people would give an arm and a leg for an opportunity like this, Shannon." Rupert's tone had cooled measurably. "You're in a good position to accept."

"Why would you say that?"

"I do my research. I know quite a bit about you."

A chill crept over her. "I don't know if I should be flattered or frightened."

"Flattered, I assure you. This could be a new chapter in your life."

She frowned, thinking about all the changes that had happened over the past year. Discovering a mother she never knew, inheriting a mansion, moving to the United States. "I'm not sure I *want* a new chapter."

He remained silent for a moment. "At least consider it."

"I will. Give me time."

"I'll expect an answer by next Monday."

"You'll have one," she assured him.

After she hung up, she bit on her lip as the conversation sank in. Maybe this *was* the right time and ideal opportunity to seriously pursue her dreams.

Or were her dreams right here in front of her?

She surveyed the kitchen around her and realized that something in the room felt different. Had Deborah rearranged something? Or maybe Michael had moved something when he came inside to check out the house.

Shannon couldn't pinpoint exactly what felt out of place, but she had the distinct feeling that something was different.

"You're being paranoid," she muttered to herself. Her imagination was going wild again. "Deborah probably did some rearranging."

Just then, Deborah wandered into the room from her small living quarters off the kitchen. In her late fifties, she had short, wavy white hair. Deborah had worked for Shannon's late grandmother for many years. Deborah had stayed on to help Shannon after she inherited the estate.

The housekeeper pulled her sweater tighter around her shoulders. "Morning, Shannon. Did I hear you talking to someone in here?"

"Good morning, Deborah." Shannon put her cup back onto the saucer. "I was just talking to myself. By chance, did you rearrange anything in here yesterday?"

Deborah's eyebrows wove together as she leaned against the kitchen counter. "No. Why do you ask?"

"Something feels different. I can't put my finger on it."

"I haven't been in here since last night. I left the house to play cards at about seven and got in shortly after eleven." Deborah gave Shannon a knowing look. "Perhaps it's all the excitement of finding that woman dead at the art show that's playing with your head."

Shannon nodded. "You could be right." She took another sip of her tea and stopped. What tasted strange about the strong brew? She drank English breakfast tea every morning.

"Your friend Michael left that tea for you last night." Deborah shuffled over to the toaster and popped in an English muffin.

Shannon paused. "Michael?"

Deborah nodded. "That's right. I found it on the doorstep yesterday evening with a note that read, 'From, Michael.' I intended on mentioning it first thing when I saw you, but you're up early this morning."

Shannon frowned. "That doesn't make any sense, Deborah. I was with Michael yesterday evening. He didn't mention anything about leaving tea on the porch. And honestly, that seems out of character for him."

Deborah turned toward her, her eyebrows scrunched together in confusion. "You're right. It doesn't make any sense."

Shannon glanced at the bottom of the cup and saw a dark substance there.

The blood drained from her face.

Could it be ... lead dust?

*       *       *

For Shannon, the next five hours were a blur. Chief Grayson came to the mansion and insisted she go to the hospital. There, she'd had a blood test, which had confirmed lead in her bloodstream—although the level wasn't high enough to be considered life threatening. She'd been given DMSA, a medication for lead poisoning, and they'd insisted she stay for observation.

Thanks to Shannon's frightening experience, the police had a pretty good idea of how someone had poisoned Sunny. Previously, they hadn't been able to figure out exactly how Sunny had been exposed to toxic levels of lead since she was always careful when she worked with it in her art studio. Now they were checking Sunny's tea.

Shannon was glad the police finally had the answer— although nearly being poisoned wasn't quite the way she'd intended to help them out.

The Purls and Essie all arrived at the hospital at the same

time and gathered around her hospital bed. Thankfully, the doctor had let Shannon keep her clothes on instead of making her change into a hideous hospital gown.

Joyce handed her a cookies-and-cream cupcake. "Cupcakes make everything better," she said.

Shannon smiled. "Yes, they do—especially yours. But I'll have to save it for later. I'm not quite ready to eat again."

Melanie patted her hand. "You take your time. We're here for you, whatever you need." She paused. "Except taste-testing your tea."

Joyce nodded. "And if they do make you change into a hospital gown, let me know. I'll jazz it up for you with some sparkly beads."

"Thank you, Joyce." Shannon grinned. "I appreciate your ability to make everything beautiful."

"What kind of monster would do this to you?" Betty asked, pacing the room. Betty and her husband, Tom, owned the Apple Grove Inn and were two of the sweetest souls Shannon had ever met. "I don't understand what this world is coming to."

"I don't know what's going on," Shannon said. "I wish I had the answers. All I can assume is that I'm getting too close to the truth, and someone doesn't like it." Shannon shrugged, perplexed.

"I heard you were shot at last night," Kate said. "I'm so glad you're OK."

"It wasn't me; it was Michael. You heard already?"

Essie nodded. "This is Apple Grove. There are no secrets."

*Except when it comes to who murdered Sunny at the town's arts and crafts festival,* Shannon thought.

"We'll get to the bottom of this," Betty said with conviction. "No one tries to kill a member of the Purls and gets away with it."

"Did someone say something about trying to kill someone?"

Their attentions swiveled toward the door. A giant bouquet of daisies entered the room. Then a head popped out to one side.

"Hunter," Shannon said, her voice guarded. Although she was happy to see him, according to Michael, the man had lied to her about who he worked for. That meant he might have lied about other things too. "Thanks for stopping by."

"Some flowers to brighten your day," Hunter said. He looked at her friends and nodded. "Ladies. Am I interrupting something?"

Her friends all adamantly insisted that he wasn't interrupting anything. A little too adamantly, in Shannon's opinion. *Would they be acting like this if they knew what Michael told me?*

"We should leave," Joyce said, pointing toward the door.

"No, no. Please stay," Hunter said. "I can only stay a moment. I was on my way to a meeting, and I wanted to bring these by for you."

Shannon took the flowers from him and put them beneath her nose before turning to Hunter. "How'd you know I was here?"

"I ran into Essie this morning while I was out jogging. I stopped by the store, but I didn't realize it was closed on Mondays. Essie hinted that something had happened." Hunter glanced at Shannon's market manager, who looked down guiltily. "Please don't be mad at her. I kept pressing for details until she finally told me where you were." His eyes shone with compassion. "Are you OK?"

Shannon nodded, that familiar weight bearing down on

her chest. "I'll be going home soon. The doctor wants to keep me for a while longer to make sure I'm OK."

Hunter took a step closer to the bed and tilted his head. "What exactly happened, if you don't mind me asking?"

Shannon wondered if Hunter already knew, if the whole conversation was just a facade. She decided to tread carefully. "Someone put lead dust in my tea."

His eyes widened. "No ..." He sounded genuinely surprised.

Shannon swallowed, her throat burning. "It's true. Apparently they're holding up to their threat that if I don't back off, I'm going to be the next victim."

"Then maybe you should heed the warning and back off."

Was he saying that because he was guilty? She shoved the thought aside. This was not the place she wanted to have a conversation about his phony company. "I can't back off now. They've irked me."

"You must be getting close enough to the truth to make someone feel intimidated."

Shannon nodded. "Perhaps."

Hunter straightened. "I know you have a lot going on, and I don't want to hold you up. I just thought flowers might make your stay here a little more pleasant."

She brought the bouquet closer. "They always do. Thank you, Hunter."

He winked and squeezed her hand. "I'll call you later to check on you, if that's OK."

Shannon couldn't help but smile. "That would be nice."

As soon as Hunter was out of the room, Melanie turned to Shannon with wide eyes. "Flowers. What a thoughtful man! And he's so handsome."

*And he might just be involved in this somehow,* Shannon thought.

"I think he could be the one," Joyce said.

"The one?" Shannon nearly choked. "I'm just now starting to accept the fact that I'm in the dating game again. I'm nowhere near ready for talk of 'the one.'"

Her friends grinned and shared a knowing look with one another. Shannon suspected they were already planning her wedding.

"We only want to see you happy," Melanie said.

"I *am* happy. I've got a good life here," Shannon said. "A *great* life, in fact. I'm not complaining."

Betty stepped closer and patted Shannon's hand. "You do have a great life. But don't ever forget that it could be even better." Betty glanced at her watch. "Speaking of which, didn't you tell me yesterday at church that you have an interview today with *The Artist's Touch*?"

Shannon slapped her forehead. "I'd totally forgotten. I should probably call and reschedule." How had she let something that important slip her mind? It suddenly occurred to her that she was also supposed to meet with Alana.

"Talk to your doctor first. See how long he's going to keep you," Betty suggested.

"Good idea," Shannon agreed.

Two more people came by to check on her—news spread quickly in the small town. If she were to leave Apple Grove to pursue bigger opportunities, she was sure she'd never find such a tight-knit community again.

What was more important—friends or a successful career? Shannon's heart told her friends, but her stubborn internal drive pushed her to see how high she could climb the ladder of success.

But dwelling on those things wasn't important at the moment. Right now, she had to focus on staying alive.

# — 11 —

Shannon was discharged from the hospital later that day, and Betty rushed her home so she had time to make herself presentable for the reporter from *The Artist's Touch*. She'd been glancing at her watch all day, ever since Betty had reminded her about the interview. She hoped to make it home in time for the meeting. Knowing her schedule would be tight, Shannon had even called Deborah and asked her to make sure that everything was suitable for company.

Betty pulled into the driveway and sat with the car idling. "You've got an hour. Are you ready for this?"

"As ready as I'll ever be." She had to get a grip. It wasn't like she was going on *Good Morning America* or something. No, this was a simple sit-down interview for a digital magazine. How hard could it be?

Betty smiled. "It certainly seems like amazing things are coming your way, Shannon—other than the poison, that is. You deserve all of these good things. I'm really happy for you. Your grandmother would be so proud."

Shannon's heart warmed. "Thanks, Betty." She stared at her friend for a moment. "That means so much to me."

"Knock 'em dead, Shannon."

Shannon chuckled. "Maybe not the best choice of words, all things considered, but thank you."

The next hour passed in a rush of activity. But when the

doorbell rang at precisely five o'clock, Shannon felt as good as new as she adjusted the funky orange scarf at her neck and smoothed her jeans.

She pulled the door open, and there stood Roberta and, behind her, a man toting a camera.

"This is quite a place you have here." Roberta's gaze roamed the house.

"Thank you. My great-grandparents built it," Shannon explained.

Roberta stared at the enormous statue in the entryway of a horse rearing on its hind legs, a snake coiled and ready to strike from below.

Shannon cleared her throat. "That was my grandmother's. I've been told she was a little eccentric."

"I like eccentric people," Roberta insisted.

They made themselves comfortable in the study, where a fire had been lit in the fireplace to ward off the chilly autumn air. Floor-to-ceiling bookcases gave the room a cozy feel and had made it one of Shannon's favorite places in the house. Deborah brought them tea—bought fresh at the store that day—as well as a plate of assorted cookies and cakes. Then they all settled in, and Roberta pressed a button on her recorder.

Hearing the beep of the RECORD button made Shannon painfully aware of everything she said. The interview started with lots of questions about Shannon's upbringing in Scotland, her family, and how she got to the States.

Roberta leaned toward her, the woman's dark eyes inquisitive. "I thought I read something about a few crimes you've solved in the area. Is that true?"

Shannon took a sip of her tea and shrugged. "I've helped out here and there."

"What do you think about the murder of that stained glass artist at the show?"

Shannon's eyebrows rose in surprise. That was the last thing she'd expected the reporter to ask about. She needed to choose her words very carefully. "I think it's a shame. Sunny was incredibly talented. The art world lost a great creative talent when it lost Sunny."

"Is it true that you discovered her body?" Roberta's intense scrutiny made Shannon squirm.

"It is. I wouldn't wish that on anyone."

"Are you investigating this case also?"

Shannon shifted again. Even if she *was* investigating, she didn't want the whole world to know about it. "I leave the real investigating to the police. I only hope to see justice served."

"I've also heard that you're being courted by R & M Designs. Can you confirm the rumor?"

Shannon's throat went dry. She had no idea the reporter would be asking so many personal questions. Where was an interruption when she needed one? "It's true that we've been speaking with each other, but nothing has been settled yet."

"Very interesting."

Shannon rubbed her hands on her jeans. "I'm curious. Where have you heard about all of this? I had no idea my life was such an open book." Would the reporter ask her about nearly being poisoned to death? She hoped not.

Roberta grinned slyly as she leaned back and crossed her legs. "I'm a reporter. I do my homework."

"I'm flattered ... I guess."

"Think of it this way. You're being talked about. That's a good thing. You want there to be a buzz about you and your work."

"I prefer the buzz to be only about my work."

Roberta shrugged. "People want a package deal nowadays. They want to know the person behind the art. The more interesting that person is, the better."

Shannon supposed that all made sense, but she still felt a little overwhelmed. "All of this interest seems so sudden."

"The art show was a big deal. More than 200 people applied and only forty got in. That's something to be proud of."

"I had no idea that many people applied. I wanted to help out a local charity. In fact, Sunny and I had talked about organizing an arts and crafts show solely as a fundraiser for local charities."

Roberta nodded. "One more thing to like about you."

Shannon took another sip of her tea, feeling a bit weak after everything that had happened. It had been a long day. Everything was starting to feel surreal.

Roberta leaned closer. "You look pale. Are you all right?"

Shannon didn't dare mention the poisoned tea. She nodded instead. "Doing great."

"Good." Roberta stood. "How about some photos then?"

They spent the next hour taking various photographs all over the house and the grounds. Then they drove to Paisley Craft Market & Artist Lofts for some snapshots in Shannon's store. Roberta was personable and inquisitive, but Shannon tried to be careful and not share too much.

Finally, it seemed as if their interview was wrapping up. Shannon was relieved. More than anything else, all she wanted to do was climb into bed and stay there until morning.

Roberta turned to her as they paused by their vehicles, parked in the lot behind the craft market. "It was a pleasure, Shannon. I really enjoyed it."

"So did I. Thanks for your interest in my work."

"Though we're a national magazine, we're based out of Portland. It's exciting to think that one of 'Oregon's own' might be hitting the big time. That's news to write about, and it's exactly what we prefer to cover at *The Artist's Touch*. We like seeing local talent find a broader market. Your work certainly speaks for itself. And your story is so interesting as well." Roberta waved her finger in the air with certainty. "You're going to make a great feature."

"I appreciate that."

As Roberta and her photographer drove off, tension pinched Shannon's spine. *Was Roberta who she'd claimed to be? Maybe I should've done more investigating before agreeing to the interview and inviting a stranger into my home.*

The woman seemed to know an awful lot about her, and the interview had opened the door to a lot of other questions. That fact left Shannon feeling unsettled.

She slipped into Old Blue, heading for home—hoping she hadn't just made a huge mistake.

\*      \*      \*

When Tuesday morning dawned, Shannon couldn't think of anything she'd like to do more than work in her shop. She was up, dressed and unlocking the door to her office by seven o'clock.

By midmorning, numerous customers had come in, all of whom had heard about her brief stay in the hospital. The store bustled with activity, and she was thankful Essie was with her to help share the workload. A good employee was priceless, a fact Shannon had realized repeatedly over the past several months.

She paused as she rearranged several craft books. It occurred to her that she hadn't heard from Michael yet. Surely he'd heard about what happened. He always heard when something happened, even when Shannon didn't want him to find out. Besides, she knew the chief had called to ask Michael about the tea anyway. *Why hasn't he stopped by?*

The bell above the door jangled. Shannon looked up with anticipation, and Erica Winters stepped inside.

She looked better today than the last time Shannon had seen her. Her hair was pulled back into a neat ponytail. She wore a crisp white shirt and fitted jeans. Her eyes, though still slightly swollen, weren't nearly as teary and red-rimmed as before.

Shannon approached the woman, depositing the out-of-place books on the counter. "Hello, Erica."

"Hi, Shannon." Her voice sounded soft as she approached Shannon. She pulled her arms across her chest, still obviously shaken by Sunny's death.

"This is a surprise," Shannon said. "What brings you out this way?"

Erica swallowed before licking her lips. "I wanted to check and see if you'd found out anything about Sunny's death. I can't sleep at night for thinking about what happened to her. It's so horrible."

Shannon shook her head, her mind racing through everything she'd learned—and the gaps still to be filled in. "I wish I could say I had answers for you. But I don't. I must be getting closer to the truth, though, because someone tried to poison me too. I spent most of yesterday in the hospital."

Erica gasped, her hand rushing to cover her mouth. "W-what do you mean?"

"Lead poisoning. In my tea." Shannon shuddered at the thought. It was a good thing she'd noticed something at the bottom of her cup. Things could have turned out much worse if she hadn't.

Erica's eyes widened, and she sagged against the counter. She drew in a long, deep breath and released it slowly. "Is that what someone did to Sunny?"

Shannon shrugged, tilting her head sympathetically. "I'm not sure. The police won't give me much information since I'm not officially part of the investigation."

A new realization trickled into her thoughts. The shooter had been a petite woman. Could it have been Erica? She would've had ample opportunity to poison Sunny, and women were more likely to poison someone than men.

*Am I looking at a killer?*

Erica shook her head, her eyes still hollow. "Maybe I shouldn't have asked you to look into this for me. It's put you in the line of danger, and that was never my intention."

"I have a feeling I was in danger before you asked me to get involved." Unfortunately, Shannon's words were true. She just didn't know *why* she was involved from the start. It had all begun with the cryptic note that someone had left at her booth right after Sunny died. She studied Erica closely. "How are you doing, by the way?"

Tears pooled in Erica's eyes. "I'm hanging in there. Everyone's been really nice. Several people from Sunny's 'artsy' circles have stopped by to offer their condolences. I guess I'm the closest thing to family that she had, so I've been the go-to person." Erica ran a finger under her eyelid to wipe away any excess moisture before straightening. "Her funeral is Friday, by the way."

Shannon leaned against the counter and tried to measure her words. "Who planned the funeral, if you don't mind me asking?"

"I don't mind," Erica said. "I planned the funeral for her. It was the least I could do." Erica dabbed beneath her eyes with a crumpled tissue.

Shannon tried to connect all of the dots. "So you have power of attorney?"

Erica shrugged. "Not officially, but there was no one else to step up. Sunny deserves a funeral. Everyone does."

"I agree. I'm sure Sunny would appreciate your thoughtfulness." Shannon shifted her weight as she wondered about the truth of Erica's words. "Another question. Sunny must have left quite a bit of wealth behind. Now that she's dead, her work will be worth even more. Who will inherit all of that?"

Erica's cheeks reddened. "I don't know. I've wondered if she left it to the artists guild or maybe one of the charities she liked so much. There was a cat rescue society that she loved."

"But you really have no idea?"

Erica shook her head. "I've only heard rumors."

"Rumors?" Shannon asked. "From who?"

"Her lawyer stopped by. I thought he was going to kick me out of the house right then and there." Erica let out a bitter chuckle and rubbed her arms.

"Why didn't he?"

"I'm honestly not sure." Erica shook her head and looked away. "All I know is that the will is being read on Thursday. He said I could stay in the house until then." She continued to avoid Shannon's gaze.

*Why was Erica reacting so strangely?*

Shannon prayed that come Thursday, maybe some answers would become apparent.

\*       \*       \*

There was a lull in customers after lunchtime, and Melanie was stocking shelves near the front of the store.

Joining her friend, Shannon leaned her head against the wall. "I'm never going to figure out what happened to Sunny."

Melanie paused from her work. "Who's your most likely suspect at this point?"

Shannon shook her head. "I'm not sure. Initially, I planned to focus on Mark Arnold and James Knight. But whoever followed me and shot at Michael on Sunday night was a clearly a female." She paused. "Erica is quickly moving to the top of my list. I hate to say it, but she's behaving suspiciously."

"Have you ever considered that maybe the person who was following you is the same person who's been leaving you those notes? Maybe it wasn't the killer at all. Maybe it was someone who was trying to feed you more information."

Shannon chewed on her words before nodding. "You know, Melanie, you might be right. That might be why she didn't actually shoot at Michael. Perhaps she missed on purpose."

Melanie nodded. "Maybe she was scared."

"If I could only catch her in the act, I might be able to get some answers. I don't know where to go next. There's this small voice in my head that keeps whispering that I should back off."

"You're good at what you do, Shannon. Be careful—but don't give up. Not when you're getting this close."

"I'm afraid I'm going to have to disagree with your friend's advice."

Shannon glanced over and saw Michael leaning against the wall near the door. She furrowed her brows at him. "Why am I not surprised?"

"Shannon, I heard about your hospital stay. You could've been killed. I would have come earlier, but my brother-in-law had a heart attack, and I was in Portland helping my sister. Are you OK?"

She nodded. "I'm fine, thank you. And I'm sorry to hear about your brother-in-law."

Michael's gaze remained fixed on her. "The incident with your tea could have been ugly. That night when I followed you home, I checked your attic and your closets. It never occurred to me there might be danger lurking in your tea."

Shannon chuckled. "That wouldn't occur to most people." She sighed. "I know you're worried, but I promise I'm going to be more careful."

He shook his head and stood up straight, his body forming a tight line. "You don't understand. There's more to this crime than you think, Shannon."

Shannon brushed flecks of glitter from her pants. "She was poisoned, that much is clear," she said. "I have the means of death, but what I don't have is the motive or the opportunity. Is there anything you can tell me in that department?"

He didn't back down, nor did his face give anything away. "You may not have it figured out as well as you think."

Her eyebrows drew together. "What exactly does *that* mean?"

"It means that things aren't always as they seem."

Her hands went to her hips. Couldn't the man ever speak plainly? Did he always have to talk in code? "Can you elaborate on that?"

"You know I'm not at liberty to say." He paused. "But I can tell you that there's more to Sunny's death than lead poisoning."

Apprehension settled between her shoulders. "Really? How much more does there need to be? Dead is dead."

He nodded, stepping toward her. "Really. I'd suggest you be careful—and that you take my advice and back off."

"Michael ...."

He reached out and squeezed her hand. "Please."

Something about the earnestness in his eyes made her want to say yes. She nearly gave in.

Instead, she pulled her hand away and went back to her office.

She had an appointment to prepare for.

\*　　\*　　\*

"Thank you for meeting with me," Alana said. She took a sip of her tea and nodded with approval. "It's always nice to find other people who prefer tea to coffee."

Shannon smiled. "Coffee's growing on me, but I'll always be a tea girl at heart."

Alana sighed. "Sunny used to love tea."

It was one more reason to make Shannon feel like they'd been kindred spirits.

Alana had graciously agreed to meet on short notice since Shannon had had to cancel their appointment on Monday, citing a "minor emergency" as the reason. She hadn't mentioned the part about someone trying to poison her.

They sat at the small table by a window in Alana's kitchen. Sunlight filtered in through gauzy drapes, and artificial geraniums smiled at them from the center of the table.

"Sunny and I used to get together every week," Alana said. "It was a great time to catch up with her. I'd hoped to be a mentor to her in life, not just a mentor in the art of stained glass."

"That's a special gift to give someone."

"Friendship *is* one of the greatest gifts, isn't it? I remember when I first moved to this area. My husband got a job as a CEO of a company—they produced pillow and mattress covers, of all things. We packed up everything and moved from Ohio to Oregon, thinking it was an opportunity we couldn't pass up."

Shannon swallowed the lump in her throat. "Are you glad you did?"

Alana shrugged. "It's hard to say. For a long time, I wasn't. I resented my husband for wanting to move. So what if we'd make more money? So what if he'd have this great new job title? What did all of that mean if you weren't around the people you loved? What did it all mean when it took you away from time with family and friends?"

Alana's words struck a chord. Shannon leaned forward. "What happened?"

"Over the years, I learned to live with the decision.

What else can one do? But I miss my family. I think all the time about moving back home, but everything has changed now. People have moved on. I can't re-create the past, unfortunately. I hope that when I'm old and gray one day, I'll have someone who wants to visit me."

"You don't have any children?"

Alana shook her head. "No. Maybe that's why I had so much time to pour myself into my art and into mentoring other people who were interested in the medium. Stained glass work has brought me a lot of joy through the years."

Would that be Shannon if she gave up her life in Apple Grove? She already had made one life-altering move. Was she ready for another? Chicago would be a long way from the twins, the Purls and her complicated, growing relationship with her mother. Would she always regret putting success over relationships? Or was she simply letting fear hold her back?

"You and Sunny must have been good friends." Shannon took another sip of her tea. "I heard she went to bat for you and insisted that you be accepted into the art show."

Alana smiled sadly. "That she did. She was intensely loyal. She didn't think it was fair that Mark acted as the sole jury for those shows."

"He was the *only* one to judge a juried art show?"

Alana nodded. "He's what some people might call a control freak." She chuckled, but it faded quickly. "No, it meant a lot to me that Sunny would do that. She was a good woman."

Shannon cleared her throat. "I have a question, Alana. I hate to change the subject, but do you have any idea who stands to inherit Sunny's business?"

Alana pursed her lips and set her tea back onto the

saucer. "Now that's an excellent question. I don't know for sure. Her parents are dead, and she has no siblings. My next guess would be that maybe a friend would inherit it."

Erica Winters flashed through Shannon's mind. But Lydia had indicated that Sunny didn't particularly care for the woman and made it seem like she had clingy tendencies.

*Clingy—or stalker-like?*

Could Erica have been the woman who'd followed her that night with Michael? Had the young accountant left the poisoned tea at the Paisley mansion before following Shannon to the diner and firing the gun? Shannon wished she had the answers.

"A friend like Erica Winters, perhaps?" Shannon ventured.

Alana shrugged. "Erica would be a good guess. They were like sisters."

"Actually, I heard they hadn't been getting along very well lately."

"They got along about as well as most women do. One minute, they seemed like best friends. The next, they were arguing. It was the cycle of their relationship. Some people are always even-tempered and steady. Others have a broad range of emotions that they freely engage."

"Brilliant observation—and so very true. We're all unique and different, aren't we?" Shannon shifted in her seat. "What do you know about James Knight? I get the impression that you don't like the man, but what else can you tell me about him?"

Alana raised her chin. "He's haughty. He knows his work is good, and he's arrogant because of it. But that's only my opinion."

"Do you think he could be capable of murder?"

"Murder is extreme. I don't know what motive he would

have had to kill Sunny." Alana thought for a moment. "It's hard to answer that question. I suspect whoever killed her has a motive that's buried deep—and it won't be easy to find."

Shannon cleared her throat. "I hate to ask you this, but I have to. I saw you put a powdery gray substance in your purse at the art show. Do you mind me asking what that was?"

Alana blinked, as if the question surprised her. "A powdery gray substance?" She reached into her purse. "You mean this?"

Shannon stared at the canister and nodded. Her throat felt dry as she waited for an explanation. "Yes, that."

"It's chalk, dear. One of my students is using it on her ceramics, and I bought this directly from another exhibitor at the show for my student to use, so she wouldn't have to pay shipping."

Shannon nearly laughed out loud, feeling ridiculous for even suspecting that Alana might be carrying powdered lead around in her purse. "Of course. I figured there was a logical explanation, and I was correct. Please excuse the silly question."

"You didn't think ..." Alana shook her head and held up her hand. "You know, it's better if I don't know."

Despite the reassurance, Shannon found herself looking at the bottom of her cup. She nearly sighed with relief when she saw the normal brown tea particles there. What had she expected? That Alana had invited her over to poison her?

"Is everything alright?" Alana asked gently.

Shannon nodded. She didn't want to admit that everyone was a suspect in her mind. But they were. Even Hunter was on her list, if she was being completely honest with herself.

She didn't like living in fear and suspicion. But when someone was trying to kill you, what choice did you have?

# — 12 —

$A$s Shannon climbed into her truck, her cellphone rang. She recognized the number as Erica's.

"Hi, Erica." Shannon jammed the phone under her ear as she cranked the engine.

A sob greeted her on the other end. "Shannon, it's terrible."

"What's terrible, Erica? Are you OK?" She leaned back in the seat. Perhaps Erica *was* a clinger, and Shannon had become her latest obsession.

"The police chief stopped by today," Erica said. "He told me that there's more to Sunny's death than they originally thought." She sobbed again.

Shannon's curiosity peaked. *Is this what Michael had hinted at?* "Can you share with me what they told you?"

She sniffled, let out a little cry, and then blew her nose. "Apparently, someone put cyanide in Sunny's water on the morning she died. Cyanide! Can you believe it?"

"Cyanide? In her water?" Shannon let her head drop back against the seat. That was news she wasn't expecting.

"The police are here going through Sunny's things right now, looking to see if there are any traces of it. They had a warrant and everything."

*Are they going through Sunny's things ... or is Erica really their target?* Shannon had a sneaking suspicion that Erica was on Grayson's radar.

143

Erica continued: "They even found traces of cyanide in the water bottle from the arts and crafts show."

Who had delivered those water bottles? Shannon remembered getting one herself. She also remembered Sunny drinking a different kind—flavored water, maybe. "I'm sorry, Erica. I don't know what to say."

"You have to figure out who did this, Shannon. You just have to!"

"I'm doing my best. Try to relax. I haven't given up." She didn't mention that Erica herself was fast becoming one of her prime suspects.

Shannon hung up and sat quietly, her head leaning against the seat for a moment. Cyanide? Perhaps the lead hadn't been working fast enough, so someone decided to speed up the process. That's the only thing that made sense.

It looked like she needed to talk to Mark Arnold again and find out who'd had their hands on those water bottles.

She glanced at her watch. She might as well pay him a visit while she was out.

But there was no way she'd drink anything that he offered.

*     *     *

Shannon pulled open the glass door of the art gallery that Mark owned. It was located in the suburbs of Portland in an artsy area. Shannon made a mental note to come back and explore the neighborhood sometime when there were less pressing matters at hand.

Mark stood looking every bit the proper proprietor at the register. He stepped forward, a cordial smile across his face. The smile disappeared when he recognized her. "Shannon McClain. What brings you this way? This is quite a jaunt from Apple Grove."

She stepped around a lovely display of pottery and stared him in the eye. "I have a few questions for you."

"You'll have to wait in line because apparently a lot of people want to speak with me. The police already talked to me. They were in here yesterday, as a matter of fact. As you can see, I'm still a free man—a guilt-free man." He spread his arms, as if showing they were unshackled.

Shannon didn't back down. "Who delivered the water bottles to the show?"

"I purchased them in bulk from a grocery store, and I had volunteers from the artists guild take turns delivering them. It's like I told the police. I can give you the names of the people who volunteer, but I didn't make a schedule of who delivered the bottles of water or when. Besides, the bottles were sealed."

"I'd like a list of the volunteers, if you don't mind."

"I already typed one on my computer for the police. I'd be happy to print you another copy, especially if that means you won't come around here harassing me again. All I need is you stirring up trouble."

"I should think you'd be more concerned about the death of one of your artists," Shannon said. "All you've seemed to care about from the start of this is your reputation."

His face reddened. "Of course I'm concerned. But I don't want to go out of business in the process. Bad publicity is a nightmare." He pushed his glasses higher on his nose. "If you'll excuse me a moment, I'll get that list."

Shannon wandered around the shop, soaking in each piece of art. She recognized some of the pieces as Sunny's and also some of the woodcarvings as James Knight's. How had the art world become this twisted? Perhaps it had always been. Art theft wasn't uncommon. Insurance fraud happened regularly. Were either of those things related to Sunny's death though? Were any of those things related to Mark?

"Here you go." Mark walked briskly toward her with a crisp piece of paper in hand. He extended it to her, the sour expression still present on his face.

Shannon took the list from him. "Thank you."

She examined the list, looking for a familiar name. Finally, she found one.

*Erica Winters.*

"You should talk to Diane Sigmund," Mark said.

Shannon blinked, wondering if the name should sound familiar. It didn't. "Who's Diane Sigmund?"

"She's the Temari ball artist who dropped out of the show at the last minute and without explanation. It's all very suspicious to me, especially when you consider that she was very excited to be a part of it. Plus, her work is phenomenal."

"How can I get in touch with her?"

He snatched the paper from her hands and jotted something on it. "Here's her number. Listen, Shannon. I want this solved as much as you do. Believe me, do I ever."

She thanked Mark and returned to Old Blue. It wasn't much, but it was something. At least she had someone else to talk to now.

An idea hit her. Was Mark Arnold Sunny's secret boyfriend?

Erica had said he lived about an hour away. That might have been Sunny's motivation for doing these shows.

Shannon shook her head. It was something to think about, and it certainly added another layer of questions to her already muddled thoughts.

*       *       *

While Shannon was in Portland, she decided she should stop by and see her children. Even though her daughter had said she might come to see her this weekend, Shannon didn't get to see the twins often enough.

She traveled around the outskirts of town until she reached the university. A moment later, she parked in front of her daughter's dorm. She didn't get out right away. Instead, she opened her phone and dialed Diane Sigmund's number.

The woman answered on the first ring. Her voice sounded older, gravelly almost, and Shannon pictured her to be the grandmotherly type. "Ms. Sigmund, I'm Shannon McClain. I was at the art show in Apple Grove this past weekend. I was hoping I might be able to talk to you about something very important when you have time."

"How about now?"

"I prefer face-to-face." Shannon had learned that reading the clues provided by body language could sometimes make or break a case.

"I suppose if you want to make the trip to see me, that would be fine. I don't take too many trips to Apple Grove."

"That wouldn't be a problem," Shannon said. "When are you available?"

"How about tomorrow morning?"

"That will be perfect."

Shannon jotted down the directions, said goodbye, and then hurried toward Lara's dorm. Her daughter answered after the first knock. Shannon's heart never failed to warm at the sight of her kids. It seemed only yesterday they were in diapers. Now, they were both grown up. Well, almost.

"Mum!" Her spirited daughter's eyes danced, and she pulled Shannon into a hug. "What are you doing here?"

Shannon laughed, delighted that her daughter was so happy to see her. There was a time not so long ago when Lara had been resentful of having her mother's presence in her life. Shannon was glad they were on good terms with each other now. "I was in the area, and I thought I'd say hi. Maybe we could all grab a bite to eat? I remember how terrible cafeteria food can be."

"That sounds great. Let me call Alec."

Shannon thought about driving to one of her mother's Gourmet on the Go food carts, but Shannon wanted to devote some undivided attention on the kids. While her relationship with Beth Jacobs had improved, it still wasn't the best. In short order, after picking up Alec outside the science building, Old Blue pulled up to a burger joint not far from campus. There, they talked about grades and friends and things they all missed about Scotland. Then Lara turned the topic of conversation to Shannon.

"What's new with you, Mum?"

Shannon shrugged. She wasn't one to talk about near-death experiences with the twins, at least not when she could avoid it. "Same old, same old."

"We heard about the lady who died at the art show," Alec said.

Shannon nodded slowly. "It was a sad day."

"I'm surprised you haven't stuck your nose into it yet," Lara said.

"Stuck my nose into it? Who do you think I am?" Shannon's voice lilted playfully.

Lara laughed. "A nosy Nelly! But we love you for it. How about other news? The shop? Your friends? There's got to be something exciting to report."

Shannon thought of Hunter and Michael. But again, there was no news there. Nothing she wanted to talk to her kids about, at least. "I'm mostly busy with work and social activities with the Purls. That's the life of your old mum, I guess."

"How's Michael?" Alec asked. He and Michael had struck up a friendship during one of Shannon's mysteries before their first semester at Portland State.

"Oh, he's fine," Shannon said, veiling her emotions. She knew Alec and Michael talked from time to time. *Does Alec know something I don't?*

"Mum, you've got to venture out of your comfort zone sometime. Live a little. Do something for *you*." Lara's voice sounded so serious that Shannon blinked with surprise. What had gotten into her daughter? Thinking about her mum and her mum's needs? Maybe her baby was growing up.

Immediately, Rupert's offer snaked through her mind. Should she take him up on that opportunity? Nothing was happening with Michael. Hunter might be lying to her about his reasons for being in her universe. Maybe she should make a clean break.

The problem with clean breaks was that they often tended to get messy—and they were never easy. This Shannon knew from experience.

"I appreciate your concern, Lara. I'll take your opinion into consideration."

The rest of the conversation was light and simple, filled with talk of classes and college life. She couldn't wait until the kids could come home to Paisley mansion for Christmas break and stay for a few weeks. That was the nice thing about living so close together.

Shannon's heart thudded with sadness again. If she moved, that wouldn't necessarily be the case. There would be more hassle involved. Even if she made more money, she wouldn't be a short drive away if the kids needed her. Of course, the twins virtually were grown and had their own lives now.

They finished lunch, and Shannon drove the twins back to campus. She found a parking spot and said goodbye to Alec before she walked with Lara to her dorm room. She wanted to measure for the new curtains her daughter had requested.

When Shannon returned to her truck, she saw something white on the windshield. The hair on the back of her neck raised as she plucked it from beneath the windshield wiper.

Before she read it, she studied the landscape around her. There were college kids everywhere. Was one of them the culprit? Had someone followed her to Portland?

Her tension grew.

She turned her focus to the words on the page: "You're on the right track. Don't give up. But be careful."

# — 13 —

Wednesday morning, Shannon knocked on the door of Diane Sigmund's quaint little cottage. A moment later, a tiny woman in her seventies answered. Her black hair, obviously dyed, was pulled into a tight bun, and her clothes were loose and flowing, almost bohemian like.

"Hello. I'm Shannon McClain."

The woman extended her hand, and Shannon instantly sensed a kindness about the woman. "Diane Sigmund. Come on in. Love your accent, by the way."

Shannon stepped inside the house, which was decorated in a Victorian style with lots of burgundy and yellow flowers. Artfully arranged in a bowl on the table were the exquisite Temari balls that Shannon had heard about.

"These are beautiful," Shannon said, almost in a whisper. She started to reach for one, but stopped. "May I?"

"You can't hurt them, dear. Go right ahead." Diane chuckled. She shuffled away a few steps, her back slightly bent with age.

Shannon examined the intricate needlework on each ball. Multiple threads looped the spheres, and designs had been stitched over the surfaces. The artistry of each piece amazed her. "These must take hours."

The older woman smiled crookedly from the doorway leading into a living area. "Some take longer than others. It depends on the design."

"How long have you been doing this?"

Diane shrugged. "It seems like forever. I read an article on them when I was a stay-at-home mom, and then I saw the pictures accompanying the piece. I was fascinated. I eventually tried my hand at it. Of course, that was probably forty years ago. My work has come a long way since then."

Shannon placed the balls back in the bowl. "I hear you're one of the best in the country."

"I don't know about that." Diane chuckled again and began walking. She motioned for Shannon to follow. "Let's go into the kitchen."

Shannon followed her through the neat house, noticing how each room had an artist's touch, with skillfully arranged hangings on the walls and lovely pillows and blankets scattered about.

Diane paused in the kitchen and pointed to a chair at a small table there. "You wanted to meet with me about the art show?"

"Yes. I was there selling my jewelry." Shannon lowered herself onto a padded kitchen chair.

Diane shuffled toward the stove. "Would you like tea?"

Would she ever be able to drink tea again without feeling a touch of fear? She swallowed before nodding. "Yes, tea please." She'd simply keep an eye on the preparation and make sure that Diane drank hers first.

As Diane set the kettle on the stove, Shannon couldn't help but notice how the woman's hands shook. The metal from the kettle clanked against the stovetop.

Diane glanced at Shannon and frowned. "You'll have to excuse me. My arthritis has been acting up lately."

The woman's fingers were swollen and knobby. Shannon

swallowed, trying to keep her voice even and unassuming. "How do you ever get all of your intricate needlework done with your arthritis?"

A strange emotion passed over the woman's face, and she turned back to the teakettle. "One stitch at a time, I suppose. Now, what did you want to talk to me about?"

Shannon rested her elbows atop a ruffled place mat. "I wanted to know why you dropped out at the last minute."

Diane shrugged and began wiping the kitchen counters. "I decided I didn't want to sit through another show."

Shannon wished the woman would make eye contact with her. There was so much truth that could be seen in someone's eyes. But Diane continued to putter around the kitchen.

"That's the only reason?"

"I'm not as young as I used to be. Those shows are a lot of work." Diane vigorously wiped the laminate countertop.

"Yes, they are. I was exhausted when everything was done. That's for sure."

Diane paused for a moment and looked over at Shannon. It appeared as though she had something she wanted to say. As quickly as the moment came, however, it ended, and she went back to her scrubbing. "My husband, Ken, used to be able to help me. But he passed away two years ago. Now it's just me."

"My husband was killed in an auto accident more than three years ago. I know how hard that can be."

Diane stopped scrubbing and looked intently at Shannon. "Why are you really here, Shannon? What do you want to know?"

There was no need to beat around the bush any more. "I'm looking into the death of Sunny Davis. I heard the competition at the show could be cutthroat. Someone suggested I talk to you and find out why you dropped out."

Diane drooped against a chair before lowering herself into it with a sigh. "Look, I don't want to start any trouble."

"I'm not trying to start trouble. I just want answers, and I was hoping you might be able to help." Shannon pleaded with her eyes, silently begging the older woman to trust her.

Diane looked from side to side before pulling her lips into a tight line. "Lately, I've been getting help with my Temari balls."

"Help?"

Diane's chin trembled. "I receive my income from those Temari balls. My Social Security won't cover all of my bills, especially since I'm still paying on my husband's medical expenses. I sell my work online and at these shows. But I've had to get someone to help me recently, with my arthritis and all."

"What do you mean by 'help'?"

Tears filled Diane's eyes as they met Shannon's. "I found someone to do the needlework for me. I still wrap the balls and do the big design elements. But someone else does the intricate needlework."

"That's a problem?"

Diane nodded. "My Temari balls have become a brand. I have collectors from all over the world that will pay top dollar for my work." She shook her head and frowned. "Even though I'm getting help, I advertise the balls as my own. I know I shouldn't, but what other choice do I have?"

Shannon's heart softened. "The ethics of that aside, what does this have to do with the show?"

Diane rubbed the place mat. "Someone found out what I

was doing. They threatened to expose me if I didn't drop out of the show. They said I could be charged with fraud."

"Why did they want you to drop out so badly?"

Diane shrugged. "I have no idea. I just know I was scared. I didn't want to go to jail or pay fines. I want to make a living."

Shannon leaned closer. "Diane, do you have *any* idea who threatened you?"

Her face twisted with anguish. "I shouldn't say."

"You should." Shannon leaned in even closer. "They essentially blackmailed you, Diane. That's illegal."

Diane sighed and looked around again. The teakettle whistled, and she jumped. Without a word, she stood and poured the water into teacups. When she sat back at the table, there was a new look of determination in her eyes.

"I'll tell you," Diane said. "But only if you promise to keep my secret."

Shannon nodded. "I promise."

Diane looked her in the eye. "It was James Knight."

\*       \*       \*

"It sounds like you have a lot of possibilities, but still no answers," Joyce said. She knit another row on a bright pink scarf she was making to send to a homeless shelter in Portland.

Melanie hadn't finished her pumpkin praline cheesecake yet, so she sat back in the plush chair and took another bite. "Many suspects are better than no suspects—right?"

Shannon nodded, happy that the Purls of Hope had decided to gather at her house for an impromptu meeting that night. Talking about the mystery with her friends was the best medicine she could ask for.

She turned her thoughts to the conversation. "I do have a lot of suspects, yet none of them completely fits the profile for the right one. That's the problem. I still haven't found the one with the motive, means, and opportunity. Everyone seems to be missing at least one of those."

Betty's knitting needles clacked together softly. She sat beside the warm fire that Shannon had started in the living room fireplace. The glow of the flames gave everything a cozy, warm feel. "How about the money? Did you follow the money?"

Shannon ran her hand down the length of the pale blue knitted blanket she was making for a cancer patient at her church. She hoped the throw would keep him warm as he fought the vile disease that was ravaging his body. "If you're talking about who stands to gain the most money from Sunny's death, no one seems to know. There's a meeting with Sunny's lawyer tomorrow night for the reading of the will. I guess we'll know after that. There are some gallery owners who will probably make a lot more money off of Sunny's work now that she's passed. But is that motive enough for murder?"

Joyce shrugged. "People have murdered over lesser things."

Shannon knit a few more rows on the blanket. "Then there's James Knight. Apparently he threatened someone in order to get her space at the art show. I can't figure out why he'd do that—why it was so important to James that the woman drop out."

Betty raised an eyebrow. "It sounds like you know where you should look next."

Shannon shook her head and drew in a deep breath. "I'm spending so much time tracking down people that I'm not spending any time at my business. The suspects in this case are spread up and down the Oregon coast, and that fact has made my schedule kind of crazy lately."

Melanie fluttered a hand in the air, the fork still nestled between her fingers as she finished her cheesecake. "You know Essie is doing a great job. You don't have anything to worry about."

Shannon knit faster. "I know. I guess I feel guilty. Besides, why am I doing this? Because of a few cryptic notes from an anonymous author asking for my help? Och, it sounds even nuttier when I say it out loud."

Joyce paused in her knitting long enough to point at her. "And because Sunny's roommate has asked you for help. Everyone knows you're good at finding answers. Too good sometimes. You're obviously making someone very nervous."

*Right. Which means my life is on the line ... again.*

Shannon readjusted her yarn. With resolve, she sighed. "Maybe I'm thinking too hard about this. Isn't the right answer usually the most obvious one?"

Betty chuckled. "Sometimes, but not always, dear. Not always."

Joyce suddenly straightened and raised her voice a decibel or two. "Enough talk about death and murder. Let's talk about something different. Let's talk about ..." she gave Shannon a pointed look. "... love."

"Sure. Who wants to talk about their love life?" Shannon asked, looping another strand of yarn around her needle. "Why don't you go first, Joyce?"

Joyce raised her eyebrows. "I'm talking about you, Shannon dear."

Shannon paused and feigned surprise. "*Me?* Well, you're going to be disappointed. There's not much to talk about here."

"I beg to differ. Two men." Joyce wiggled two fingers in the air. "Two handsome men are chasing after your heart."

"They're hardly chasing after me."

Betty leaned closer, her eyes wide with curiosity. "Tell us about that Hunter fellow."

Shannon filled them in on everything she knew about him. "Michael claims the company Hunter said he works for doesn't exist." Shannon hadn't exactly meant to say those words out loud, but the thought was still nagging at her. Now she'd managed to turn the conversation topic back to mystery and mayhem.

Melanie's mouth gaped open. "Michael looked into Hunter's background?"

Shannon nodded. "Apparently."

Joyce snorted. "Don't tell me Michael's not interested in you."

"He's just being Michael," Shannon said. "He's an investigator, so he's doing what he does. He's ... he's following a hunch, I suppose." Shannon continued to knit faster and faster until she realized she needed to stop and rework part of her stitches.

Betty paused to take a sip of her coffee, never taking her eyes off Shannon. "Did you ask Hunter about his company?"

Shannon shook her head, giving up on knitting for a moment. "Not yet. It's an awkward subject to raise, especially if I don't want him to think I've been looking into his background. Exactly how do I approach that?"

"He could have a perfectly logical explanation." Melanie's voice sounded doubtful.

Despite that, Shannon nodded with gusto. "Exactly."

"Or maybe he doesn't," Joyce chimed in.

Shannon sighed. Why wasn't anything in her life simple?

# — 14 —

As Shannon approached her store on Thursday morning, she was surprised to see a familiar figure standing on the sidewalk in front of the door.

James Knight.

He paced the walkway, his hands stuffed deep into the pockets of his carpenter jeans. A scowl pulled across his face, his lips moved as if he were having an internal conversation with himself—a conversation that appeared to be heated.

Shannon tensed at the sight. Was he here to threaten her? She paused at the corner, unsure if she should come any closer. Her hand riffled through her purse until her fingers wound around her cellphone.

Maybe she should call the police. Maybe she should call Michael ....

Just as she started to pull the phone out, James spotted her. "Shannon!"

Her grip on the phone tightened along with every muscle in her neck. She left her hand inside her purse, despite how strange she must look. She'd take looking strange to ending up dead.

Something snorted near Shannon's foot, and she let out a small scream.

"Sorry, Shannon," Kate chuckled as she passed by with four dogs on leashes. "Sheesh, how much coffee did you drink this morning?"

Shannon watched as the offending mutt slobbered and walked on. "Too much, apparently."

"Catch you later," Kate called out as the dogs pulled her forward.

*Good. Someone saw me talking to James. Kate, relay that to the police if I mysteriously disappear.*

"James." Shannon kept her voice even, unwilling to show her fear. But she didn't move any closer to the man. Instead she remained under the street lamp, beside an oversized pot of pansies. "What brings you here?"

"I wondered if I could speak with you for a moment." His face softened, and his earlier craziness faded. He didn't look like the cocky artist anymore. He looked hurt and vulnerable.

Shannon's hand remained on her phone. She had to be sensible. The man had blackmailed a sweet, seventy-year-old woman and cheated her out of additional income. It didn't matter how vulnerable he looked. The man could still be dangerous.

"What do you wish to speak about?"

"Sunny." James said, eyes pleading with her. "I promise it won't take long."

Shannon wasn't about to let him into her store, not when it meant she would be alone with him inside the building. At least outside on the sidewalk there might be witnesses if he turned aggressive. "Fine. But we're talking out here."

"OK." James heaved a deep breath and took a few steps toward her. "I don't really know where to start, so I guess I'll just jump in. Sunny and I were dating."

Shannon stared at him. It took a moment for his words to sink in. "Dating?"

He nodded and rubbed a hand across his neat beard. "We were keeping it hush-hush. We didn't want anyone to know. But remember those notes that you said someone saw us passing at the art show last weekend? We didn't think anyone would catch on. She'd dropped her phone and broken it, so we couldn't text each other like we usually did. We thought it would be fun to actually write notes and pass them to each other. It made us feel like we were kids again."

"Dating?" Shannon repeated again. Originally, she'd guessed James to be much older than Sunny, but now that she got a better look at him, she realized that despite his graying hair, his skin was smooth, and his build was lean.

"I know this might come as a surprise, but we really loved each other. It breaks my heart that she's gone." Tears welled in his eyes. "Truly, she was my soul mate."

"How long did you date?" Shannon kept her guard up, unwilling to be bowled over by compassion.

"Six months."

"I heard she'd just broken up with someone. To be precise, that someone had just broken up with her."

Anguish stained his eyes. "It's true. I did break up with her for a short while, but then I realized I was simply jealous—resentful of her passion for her work. I felt second best at times. But I decided that I'd take second best to nothing at all. I begged her to give me another chance, and she did."

The pieces still weren't fitting together in Shannon's mind. What was James not telling her? "You say that you were keeping your relationship with Sunny quiet. Why would you want to keep that secret?"

He rubbed his beard. "Sunny was a very private person.

I'd just broken up with someone else right before we started dating the first time, and that complicated things. Sunny and I *were* planning to announce that we were a couple, maybe at Christmastime." A tear spilled from his eyes and soaked into his beard. "That will never happen now."

Shannon squelched her compassion, not wanting to let her heart get in the way. As she watched another tear roll down his cheek, cutting off her emotions became increasingly difficult. "Why did you threaten Diane Sigmund so that she would to drop out of the show?"

James eyes widened. He swiped a finger under his eye in one quick stroke. "I didn't threaten Diane. I didn't even know she was supposed to be in the show."

Shannon shook her head, knowing that what he was saying differed from what Diane had told her. "She said you threatened to spill one of her secrets unless she dropped out."

The woodcarver adamantly swung his head back and forth. "No way. I don't threaten people. Besides, I hardly know the woman. I certainly don't know any secrets about her."

"She claims you did."

"Then she's confused. Maybe you should talk to her again. Her work isn't in direct competition with mine. Her being at the art show—or not being there—didn't affect me in the least."

Shannon considered the point. Whose work *did* Diane's presence effect? That was the question to be answered. Her grip on her cellphone loosened. "Why did you feel the need to share this with me, James?"

His cheeks reddened. "Because the police are asking questions, and they're not getting any answers. I need to know what happened to my Sunny. I knew you were 'unofficially' looking into the matter also."

Shannon nodded. "A friend of hers asked me to see what I could find out."

"I would never hurt her." His voice changed from friendly to passionate. "Do you understand that? Never!"

Shannon took a step back—fear rippling through her. "I hear you."

*        *        *

James hadn't stuck around—thank goodness. As he disappeared down the street, Shannon slipped into the store, leaving the front door locked for a few minutes longer than necessary.

Her heart pounded in her ears. Had she just been staring into the face of a guilty man? She couldn't be sure. Her conclusions fluctuated between belief in his grief to conviction in his guilt. Could both be true? Could he be both guilty *and* grieving? If so, why would he have wanted Sunny dead?

Perhaps James was a scorned lover. It's possible he didn't break up with Sunny at all—maybe she broke up with him, and Erica had her facts wrong. There were so many questions and so few answers.

The business day began, and Shannon stayed busy with work. Essie had to take time off to work on a commissioned sidewalk art piece in Portland, so Shannon was on her own.

As soon as there was a lull between customers, she checked her cellphone for messages. She saw that she'd missed two calls from Hunter. Her heart twisted as she realized that, for some reason, she was resistant to calling him back. It had to be because of what Michael had told her. She needed to ask Hunter about the company he worked for and get to the bottom of the issue.

She sighed as she found herself dialing Diane Sigmund's number instead of Hunter's. Perhaps she needed a little more time to mull over how best to broach the topic with him.

Diane answered on the first ring, and Shannon reminded Diane who she was.

"Yes, Shannon. How are you?"

"I'm fine." Shannon continued, dusting one of the shelves. "I have a question for you. You said James Knight threatened you in a note. How do you know he's the one who wrote it?"

"He signed his name to the paper."

Shannon paused. "He handwrote the threat?"

"No. The notes are typed, signatures and all."

Shannon stared at the red glitter that now coated her fingertips. "Do you still have the letters?"

"Of course I do."

"May I see them?"

"Only if you promise not to show them to anyone. I could get in a lot of trouble."

Shannon waved to a customer who entered the store. Why did the girl look so familiar? She couldn't place her right now, so she turned her attention back to Diane. "The last thing I want to do is get you in trouble, Diane. I just want to see the notes—see if there are any clues in them."

"Like I said, they're all typed, dear. I'm not sure how much help it's going to be."

Shannon bit on her lip. "I don't know. Maybe I'm grasping at straws, but I've got to explore every option."

"Tell me when you're coming, and I'll have them ready for you. How's that?"

Some of the tension eased from Shannon's muscles. "That sounds perfect. Let me look at my schedule, and I'll get back with you."

She hung up just as the girl who'd entered the store came to the register. Shannon tried not to widen her eyes too much when she saw the girl was purchasing stained glass art supplies. *Casual, Shannon. Stay casual.*

Shannon cleared her throat and smiled. "Are you just learning stained glass, or have you been doing it for awhile?"

"I've been doing it for a few months now." The girl's voice sounded barely above a whisper. She was mousy—a petite build and light brown hair. Shannon guessed her to be in her late teens or early twenties.

"Are you enjoying it? I've considered trying my hand at it for a while now."

The girl shrugged her bony shoulders, the action making her look even frailer. "It's something to do."

Shannon gave her the total. The girl pulled cash out of her wallet, dashing Shannon's hopes of learning her identity the easy way.

"You know," Shannon said, "we have lofts upstairs that we rent out to artists. If you're interested, let me know."

The girl nodded, but said nothing.

Shannon tried harder. "In fact, if you leave your name, I'll add you to our mailing list, so you can stay up to date on everything. The space is limited, so you have to grab it while it's available."

"That's OK." The girl raised her bag and offered a small wave. "Have a good day."

She slipped out the door before Shannon could think of another excuse to get her name.

Had Shannon just let a potential lead walk out the door?

*       *       *

At nine o'clock on Thursday night, Shannon dialed Erica's number. Patience never was one of her strongest traits, and that was proving itself true again. All the runaround Shannon was getting everywhere she turned was beginning to pull at her already sore nerves.

When the woman answered the phone, Shannon could hear the catch in her voice. "Erica? It's Shannon McClain."

"Oh, Shannon. I was going to call you!" The woman sounded panicked.

Shannon pulled her legs under her as she sat on the couch in her living room. She willed herself to remain calm. "What's wrong, Erica?"

Erica sniffled. "I don't know where to start."

"The beginning? Isn't that what they always say?" Shannon tried to keep her voice light, but her effort didn't work.

"They read Sunny's will tonight. She left me her house, as well as part of her money."

Shannon quickly tried to process the new information—and the potential implications that came with it. "That's good news, right?"

Erica blew her nose. "She must have added me to her

will before we started arguing about everything. You see, I lost my job a few months ago. If Sunny had kicked me out like she was threatening to do, then I wouldn't have had anywhere to go."

"Kicked you out?" Shannon feigned surprise at Erica's confession. "Would she really do such a thing?"

"Not the Sunny I used to know. But she'd been acting strange in the months before she died. Everything I did irritated her. I'm not sure where things went wrong."

"Are you afraid the police will think you're guilty?"

Erica let out a sob. "They *already* think I'm guilty. They're here right now, searching for evidence."

Shannon straightened, the twist in the conversation causing adrenaline to rise in her. "On what grounds?"

"They asked me if they could. They said they'd get a warrant otherwise, so what choice did I have? Oh, Shannon, I think they're going to arrest me!"

"I'm coming over. Don't talk to them until I get there. Promise?"

Erica whimpered again. "I'll try not to …."

Shannon grabbed her purse, ran outside, and jumped into her truck. She had to force herself to not speed on her way to Erica's.

Three police cars were parked outside the house when she arrived. She threw her truck into park and ran to the front door. Erica came to the door with tear-rimmed eyes.

"Are you OK?" Shannon asked.

Erica shook her head. "No. The police found cyanide in one of our cookie jars. I didn't put it there, Shannon. I promise you I didn't!"

# — 15 —

Shannon couldn't help but notice that Erica was missing from the funeral on Friday.

It was because she was locked in jail, unable to post bail.

The night had been long and agonizing. The police had questioned Erica until she became hysterical and could no longer talk. Then Chief Grayson arrived with an arrest warrant. Shannon wanted to plead Erica's innocence for her, but she couldn't seem to find the words. Instead, she comforted Erica and tried to calm her. All the while, she was thinking, What if Erica really did kill Sunny? The evidence was certainly stacked against the woman. But for some reason, a sliver of doubt had lodged itself in Shannon's mind.

She shifted in the wooden pew at the church and pulled her black sweater more snugly around her.

Melanie gently sat beside her and put an arm around Shannon's shoulders. "I thought you could use company."

"I appreciate it. Funerals aren't exactly my activity of choice," Shannon said with a grimace.

Melanie frowned. "No one likes a funeral. I didn't know Sunny, but I thought you could use the support."

Shannon hugged her friend. "Thank you."

"I know you'd do the same for me." Melanie offered an encouraging smile.

Melanie was right. Shannon would always do whatever

she could to support her friends. They'd been there for her more than once. She was so grateful to have such a wonderful circle of ladies who'd supported her throughout everything that had happened since she'd inherited the Paisley mansion and the craft market.

Shannon's phone played a cheerful tune in her purse. She gasped and fumbled with her purse as several people turned to give her looks of disapproval. "Sorry," she mumbled.

Finally she found her phone and glanced at the screen. It was Hunter. She switched the phone to silent mode. She needed to talk to him, but now definitely wasn't the time.

"Did you ask him about the company he said he worked for yet?" Melanie whispered. She'd clearly seen his name on the caller ID.

Shannon shook her head, ignoring a few people who continued to glare at her. "Haven't had the chance."

"Don't let a silly misunderstanding come between you."

Shannon nodded. "You're right. I'm being ridiculous. A simple conversation will clear the air, I'm sure."

They both turned and watched as more people filed into the sanctuary. There was a good turnout from the arts and crafts community.

Shannon leaned toward Melanie, keeping her voice low. "Did you hear that Erica was arrested?"

Melanie nodded. "Betty told me. At least the bad guy—or girl, I should say—is behind bars—right? And right in time for the funeral. May Sunny's soul rest in peace."

"Right." But even as Shannon said the words, she had a hard time believing them. Why was she so hesitant to believe that Erica was guilty?

Instead, she peered at the people in the pews around her. Could the real person behind the murder be among them? There certainly was no shortage of suspects. Mark Arnold was in attendance. But a prickly personality didn't necessarily equate to murder. James Knight stood near the door as though ready to bolt. He'd claimed that he and Sunny had been dating, but was there something more to the story?

Shannon thought about the cyanide being found in Sunny's blood and her home. Who could easily get their hands on the substance? And who would have had the opportunity to leave it at Sunny's house? Erica had mentioned that several people from Sunny's circle of artsy friends had stopped by to offer their condolences, but Shannon hadn't thought to ask who.

I need to get those names from Erica.

Shannon had spent Thursday night investigating cyanide online and had tried to narrow her suspect list based on who might have had easiest access to the product. She'd discovered that cyanide could either be found in gas or crystal form, and that it was often used in manufacturing things such as paper, plastics, and textiles.

Alana Golden slid into the pew on the other side of Shannon. Her face was lined with grief as she untangled a forest green scarf from around her neck and placed it atop her purse on the bench. "This is a day that I never thought would come," she said quietly to Shannon.

"A life gone too soon," Shannon said. "It's a tragedy."

"Yes, it is. And the person responsible needs to be brought to justice." Alana's expression hardened. "Speaking of which, there's someone I want to talk to you about."

Alana hadn't heard that there'd been an arrest? Shannon started to tell her, but stopped. "Who's that?"

"A student of mine. Her name is Laura Applebee."

"You think she's responsible for Sunny's death?" Shannon whispered.

Alana looked to the left and right before nodding. "She's been acting suspicious lately. Last week, she stopped coming to class at my house."

"You taught her stained glass technique?"

Alana nodded. "I did. She had promise, if she would get her head out of the clouds. That mousy little girl is as flaky as they come."

Shannon's spine clinched as puzzle pieces began to come together in her head. "Mousy? What exactly does the girl look like?"

"Young," Alana said. "She's twenty, but she could easily pass for younger. She has light brown hair, and she's shy."

The girl who recently came into my shop to buy stained glass supplies. "Where can I find this Laura Applebee?"

"She likes to hang out at that bakery in Apple Grove."

"The bakery in Apple Grove?" Shannon asked. "You mean Pink Sprinkles?"

Alana nodded. "Yes, that's the one."

"Does Laura live in Apple Grove?"

"No. I'm not sure what her fascination with the town is. She always seemed to be traveling there for one reason or another."

Shannon couldn't help but think the police had arrested the wrong person.

\*        \*        \*

After the funeral, Melanie had to hurry back to work, which left Shannon by herself.

Shannon reached for her purse beneath the bench and grabbed a green scarf instead. Alana's. She must have dropped it when she got up to leave.

Shannon folded the soft material and put it in her bag, intending to drop it off later. She needed to head out that way and pick up the blackmail letters from Diane anyway. She decided she'd stop by Alana's on the way back.

Alana had sacrificed a lot while her husband moved up the corporate ladder. Maybe she'd have advice for Shannon about her tempting job offer.

James approached her as she pulled her coat on by the front door. "I heard the police made an arrest," he said. "Thank goodness. Maybe I can finally sleep at night, knowing someone will pay for Sunny's death."

"Speaking of the arrest, did you know Erica?"

James's eyebrows flickered toward the ceiling as people filed out the door beside them. "I only knew what Sunny told me about her."

"And what did Sunny tell you?"

He shrugged and rubbed his beard. "Only that she was a bit of a lost soul. She was prone to depression and anxiety, and couldn't seem to hold a commitment for the life of her."

"Did she and Sunny get along well?"

He shrugged again before nodding. "I suppose. Most of the time, at least. When Erica wasn't in one of her emotional vortex states, she was the best kind of friend to have around. She was fun, a good listener, there when you needed her. But when Erica got down, she became needy and insecure—and desperate."

"I heard that Sunny left her the house. Does that surprise you?"

James shook his head. "Not really. Sunny liked to take care of people. I'm sure she couldn't stand the thought of Erica being homeless. Besides, she probably wrote that will a year ago when things were all … sunny." He frowned as he said the last word.

"It's strange, considering that they'd been bickering so much."

"They were still friends. Sure, they drove each other crazy, but they'd been friends for so long that nothing was going to break their bond. They were practically like sisters."

Since James seemed to be in a chatty mood, Shannon asked, "Do you know to whom or where any of Sunny's other belongings were left?"

"Most of them she donated to various charities."

Shannon eyed Mark Arnold from across the room. "Did any of it go to the artists guild?"

"I couldn't tell you. I don't remember, to be honest. You'd have to ask Mark. I can't imagine she'd want to help that man out."

"How about you? Did you benefit from her death in any way?" Shannon knew her words sounded harsh, but she felt like she needed to ask.

James's cheeks reddened again. "I believe the person who killed her is behind bars, Shannon. Now, if you'll excuse me, I've had enough of your insinuations."

As he stomped away, Shannon saw Mark walking away. Time to make someone else angry ….

\*       \*       \*

"I assumed since someone had been arrested that you'd stop with your nosy questions. I can see that's not the case." Mark's nostrils flared.

Shannon had caught up to him right outside the door. "You heard there was an arrest also? News spreads fast."

"In our circles, it certainly does." He pushed his wire-framed glasses higher on his nose. "We're all relieved, to be honest. At least it wasn't someone in the art world. Artists have enough problems without adding a killer into the mix."

"Enough problems?"

He shrugged impatiently. "You know, competitiveness, moodiness, prone to addiction."

"You've got to be kidding me."

He pursed his lips. "It's a proven fact that artists generally have a certain type of temperament. Like it or not, the facts are documented."

Shannon decided to let the issue drop. "Did Sunny leave you any money?"

His eyebrows shot up. "You're direct, aren't you? And to answer your question—no, she did not. I didn't expect her to. It was no secret we didn't see eye to eye."

There went his motive for murder.

He harrumphed and crossed his arms. "I don't know why I'm about to tell you this since you've acted like nothing but a sworn enemy since the day we met. But I wanted to mention that you've got a real eye for design. Your jewelry is impressive, and I was thrilled to have you as a part of my show."

His compliment nearly left her speechless. "Well, thank you."

He nodded curtly. "You're welcome." He turned on his heel and walked away.

Shannon examined the crowd again, but she didn't see anyone else she needed to chat with. It seemed that everyone respected Sunny, but very few people really knew her. Was that the price of success?

She walked away from the church and headed down the sidewalk. She'd parked in a lot a block away to allow more parking spaces for artists and friends from out of town. The day was chilly, but with her coat and scarf, she was still comfortable.

She rounded the corner of the bank, nearing the parking lot beyond the building where she'd parked her truck. That's when she saw a figure in black running away from Old Blue.

It was her.

The woman who'd shot at Michael.

Shannon had to catch her—and now.

# — 16 —

Chasing after the mysterious woman, Shannon raced past parked cars, SUVs, and a truck. But the woman had too much of a head start. Shannon's legs burned as she sprinted with every ounce of her strength. Her lungs screamed for air, but she continued to push herself.

She tried to get a hint as to who the woman was, but the all-black attire and hat didn't allow for detailed observation.

As Shannon rounded another car, her ankle twisted and sent her crashing to the ground. Her knees and palms scraped the rough asphalt, and she gasped with pain. High heels had never been ideal for chasing people, no matter how easy the movies made it look.

Shannon sagged against someone's car and rubbed her ankle. It wasn't sprained, but it was going to hurt.

Even worse, the woman had gotten away. Shannon resisted the urge to scream in frustration. Instead, she pulled herself to her feet, hobbled to her truck, and plucked the paper from the windshield. It read: "You're getting closer. Don't give up."

*Thanks a bunch,* she thought. *Why can't the woman simply tell me who to look for? That would make this so much simpler.*

"Shannon, are you OK?"

She looked up. Michael stood next to Old Blue, his eyebrows

scrunched together in concern. Great—he'd stumbled upon another of her less-than-flattering moments.

"I was driving past and noticed you leaning against your truck."

She plastered on a smile as he grabbed her elbow and helped her steady herself.

"I suppose you could say I'm fine." She showed him the paper. "I got another note."

He took the paper. Shivers raced up her arms when she got a whiff of his spicy aftershave. *Och! I'm too old for this.*

"Did you see who left it?"

Shannon nodded. "It was the woman I was chasing before my heel had an unfortunate run-in with a crack in the asphalt and I ended up on the ground. She was dressed like the person who shot at you the other day."

"Is your ankle sprained?"

"Not my ankle, only my pride."

His ever-perceptive eyes glanced at her ankle. "Aside from this hiccup, how's your investigation going?"

"Great," she said, her voice flat. "Every day, I end up with more questions than answers."

"The answer to find, first the right questions you must ask." The side of Michael's lip curled up in a smile.

"OK, Yoda. Thanks for the advice." She knew it was good advice, despite his fortune cookie–style cadence.

"I hear Grayson made an arrest," Michael said.

"I think he arrested the wrong person."

Michael's eyes clouded with concern. "Please be careful, Shannon."

She nodded. "I will. I promise—no dark alleys, no isolated

meetings with strangers, and no soldering my jewelry without protective wear."

A hint of a smile crossed his lips. He nodded toward his car, parked along the street in the distance. "I've got a meeting to run to. Let me help you into your truck first."

She didn't bother to try and refuse, knowing it would do no good. He took her arm, gallantly opened Old Blue's door, and waited until she was seated in the front seat before offering a wave goodbye.

She stared down at the note that she had placed on the seat beside her. *I'm getting closer, huh?* That could mean one of several things, and that could still leave numerous suspects. Today she'd questioned James Knight and Mark Arnold. Had the mystery woman been watching?

One thing was for certain. Whoever was leaving the notes knew that Erica Winters wasn't guilty. Nor was Erica the mysterious woman who'd been leaving the notes. The police had arrested the wrong person. But Shannon would need solid proof before Chief Grayson would listen to her.

She thought about driving to Alana's to return the scarf, but she needed to stop by the store first. They'd been especially busy lately, and Shannon knew that Essie and the part-timers couldn't handle all of the responsibilities alone. Melanie had been coming in to help too, but she also had another job.

As Shannon started down the road, she wondered what it would be like to design jewelry full-time—to not have to worry about staffing the store or Espresso Yourself, to be able to concentrate solely on her art, to wear power suits, to be involved in the social scene, and to have her name become a household brand.

The exciting thoughts raised mixed emotions. On one hand, it would be a relief to be able to focus on doing the thing she loved most—creating. On the other hand, she'd miss the community around her.

Decisions, decisions. She'd told Rupert that she'd call him back first thing next week. That meant she only had a couple more days to figure out the rest of her life. The answers were still no clearer—about her future or Sunny's murder.

She pulled up to the Paisley Craft Market and gingerly limped inside. There were six people waiting in line, and Essie looked ready to pull her hair out.

Investigating would have to wait until later. Right now, she had a business to run.

\*         \*         \*

As soon as the store closed, Shannon made herself a latte and sank into one of the plush chairs in the coffee area. She propped her feet on the table and closed her eyes. *What a day.*

Two of her part-timers had called in sick. Shannon had intended to work on online jewelry orders, but there'd been no time. That meant the next day would be extra busy as well.

Just as she'd begun to relax, her phone rang. She glanced at the number on the screen. It was her mother.

"Hi, Beth."

"Shannon, how are you? It's been awhile since we last talked, and I wanted to check in."

"I'm hanging in, I suppose."

"I heard about the murder at the art show."

"Word gets around, huh?"

"It was on the news. I was in Apple Grove a few days ago and overheard a couple of people at Grandma May's talking about it too. I stopped by the craft market to say hi, but Essie told me you'd taken a drive up the coast. Sorry I missed you. Perhaps we could do dinner sometime?"

"Dinner would be lovely. I'd like to hear how you're doing." There was a lot of lost time to compensate for, and there was so much she still didn't know about her mother. Shannon had enjoyed hearing stories about her mother during their years apart. Now that she understood that Beth had disappeared in an attempt to keep Shannon and her father safe, the wounds of abandonment were healing. She had been able to get a better picture of who her mother was.

Which brought her thoughts back to the job offer in Chicago. It would mean putting more distance between her and her mother, which would only make their new relationship that much more difficult to build. Her heart twisted at the thought.

"Let's plan on it sometime next week," Shannon suggested. By then, she'd have given Rupert a final answer about his job offer.

They talked for a few more minutes about Lara and Alec, how things were going at the store, and plans for the upcoming weekend.

She'd just hung up when she heard someone knock at the front door of the store. *Who could that be? We're closed.*

A moment later, Essie peered around the corner. "Your friend is here, Shannon. Do you want me to let him in?"

Shannon glanced around the corner and saw Hunter on the other side of the glass. She had to talk to the man again eventually. Ever since Michael had shared his findings with her, she'd put distance between herself and Hunter. That wasn't fair, considering the man could have a reasonable explanation for everything.

"Yes, please. And would you mind straightening the front for me? My ankle is sore, and I could use a rest."

"No problem." Essie unlocked the door, let Hunter in, and then locked it behind him.

Shannon motioned for Hunter to come into the coffee shop area. "Hello, Hunter."

"I intended stop by earlier, but I got absorbed in my work. You'd just closed when I arrived, so I ventured to see if you might open for me." He grinned. He was handsome—any woman would think so. But charm could be deceptive and beauty fleeting. Wasn't that how the saying went?

"Have a seat." Shannon pointed to a chair.

He continued standing. "I was wondering if you'd had dinner yet."

She hadn't eaten since lunch. "As a matter of fact, I haven't."

"Then I was hoping you might have dinner with me."

Maybe dinner together would give her the chance to ask him a few probing questions without seeming too nosy. "Sure, that sounds great. Somewhere close, if that's all right. My ankle is a tad sore."

"Everything OK?"

She grimaced as she lowered her foot to the floor. "Just twisted it earlier. I'll be fine."

"How about Granny May's down the street then?"

Shannon smiled. "That would be perfect."

He helped her to her feet. She took a moment to steady

herself before hobbling toward the front door. "Essie, will you be OK here by yourself? I'll stop by after dinner and do anything else that needs to be done. I know today was crazy busy."

"I'll be fine. You take it easy, Shannon."

Walking to Grandma May's was a slow process. As they entered the restaurant, it struck Shannon as comical that they were headed to the very place where Michael had told her his puzzling news about Hunter's nonexistent company. Now here she was with Hunter.

They chose a corner table and ordered the dinner special: pot roast and potatoes. The meal was heavier than what Shannon usually liked, but her appetite at that moment was ferocious.

"How has your week been going?" Hunter asked, his eyes connecting with hers.

She shrugged. "I can't complain, I guess. I've been staying busy. How about you? How's work?"

"Busy also."

"Are you making headway on your research?"

"Yes. I've really enjoyed being out in the field and observing the rockfish in action. I'm hoping this research will help us to understand the species better. The more we understand them, the more we can predict their migratory patterns, and therefore we can learn how to keep them from becoming endangered."

"Fascinating," Shannon said, trying to sound believable. "So, who did you say you worked for again?"

"I'm here on business with Bayside Marine Research Associates." Hunter didn't seem the least bit annoyed that he had told Shannon this before. "I also teach part time at Lawson College, although I'm on sabbatical while I'm on this assignment."

"This Bayside Marine company ... how did you get a job with them? Were they your dream employer?"

He shrugged. "I don't know if I'd call them my dream employer, but they certainly have been good to work for. They allowed me to write the grant proposal for this project because they knew it was one that interested me and that it could help the environment."

"Where is the company headquartered?" Shannon tried to keep her voice casual and make her questions seem more inquisitive than like the interrogation they were meant to be.

"In Southern California." He tilted his head. "You're asking a lot of questions. If I didn't know better, I'd think I was one of your suspects." He chuckled, and Shannon realized with relief that he was joking.

She laughed too. "I was just curious. I know my husband got a couple of grants when he worked as a geologist. I wondered how similar your jobs were."

"I'm sure they're similar in many ways."

The waitress arrived with their food. The savory aroma of beef and vegetables and gravy rose to meet her with the steam. Her stomach grumbled, letting her know it was ready for food.

*Good timing for my stomach,* she thought. *But bad timing for the conversation.*

Would she ever get to the truth now?

\*       \*       \*

Saturday morning, Essie and Melanie were both scheduled to work in the store. Though Shannon knew she absolutely had to be there later in the day, she decided to take a trip to get the blackmail letters from Diane Sigmund first. She desperately wanted to get some answers and put the investigation behind her.

She'd nearly come to the conclusion that she'd done all that she could do. Unless one of her leads panned out soon, she'd be left spinning her wheels. If the crazy woman who was following her and leaving notes thought that someone else was guilty, who was to say that woman was right? Maybe she simply enjoyed playing games with Shannon's head. Maybe she had some other deeper, darker motives.

Lost in thought, Shannon flipped on her turn signal. Real life was waiting for her while she nosed around town, asking questions. She needed to reorder product at the store. An artist had destroyed one of the walls while doing an art project in one of the loft studios, and it needed to be repaired. She had several online orders for necklaces she had yet to find the time to create.

For a single woman with two kids away at college, she certainly had a full schedule.

The rain started up as she drove northward. Rain always made her think of her native home. Scotland had more than its fair share of cold, rainy days. Though she enjoyed the sunshine, she'd never been bothered by gloomy weather.

*I wonder what the weather's like in Chicago?*

The thought reminded her that she still needed to make up her mind so she could call Rupert back and give him an answer. But what should she tell him? Of course she wanted to be successful. But how did one define success?

Finally, she turned off the highway, traveled a few back

roads, and reached Diane's little cottage. Before Shannon knocked at the door, it opened.

Diane greeted her with a smile. "Good to see you, Shannon. Come in."

"I appreciate you letting me stop by." Shannon stepped inside and wiped her feet on the mat.

"No problem at all. Wait right here, and I'll go get them." Diane shuffled toward the back of the house and disappeared.

A moment later, she returned with a handful of white papers. The edges were wrinkled, as if they'd been handled too much. Shannon wondered if Diane sat to read them often, stressing out all the while.

She thrust them toward Shannon with a frown pulling on her lips. "Here they are. As you'll see, they're signed 'James Knight.'"

*If James had blackmailed someone, certainly he'd be smart enough not to use his real name.* The man was no dummy. He would certainly know how to be more subtle than that. More than likely, someone had signed his name in an effort to implicate him.

Shannon leaned against the wall and opened one of the folded pieces of paper. She read the words typed on the page:

"You're a fraud. Your work isn't your own. Back off or else. —J.K."

She looked at the next letter in the stack:

"Once people find out what you're doing, your reputation will be ruined. Drop out of the show next weekend, or I'll expose your secret. —James"

Then the next one:

"If your reputation is ruined, then you'll have no business.

Better to stay quiet and fed than to do the show and lose everything. —You Know Who"

Shannon shook her head. She didn't approve of what Diane was doing, but whoever sent the letters was downright nasty. They'd known the woman was tight on money and exploited it. The notes had probably taken years off her life, for that matter.

"I almost wish I'd never made a name for myself," Diane muttered.

Shannon glanced at Diane, the statement catching her off guard. "What do mean?"

"I mean that all of this crafting and artistry used to be fun when I was only doing little art shows. Success comes at a price."

"What kind of price?"

"For me? Pressure. What I used to love doing became a job, and it sucked away all of my joy."

Shannon would have to think about that later. As much as she'd like to chew on it now—especially with her big decision quickly approaching—she really needed to concentrate on the letters at the moment.

"How did you receive these letters, Diane? In the mail?"

Diane shook her head. "Someone stuck them under my door."

"Do you have any idea how someone could've found out that the Temari balls you made weren't exclusively your work?"

"I've thought about that. The only person who knows is the girl who helps me with the Temari balls."

"And who is she?"

Diane's face twisted with regret, and she wrung her

hands together. "She's actually my granddaughter. I taught her this art from a very young age and instantly recognized that she had talent. She's so artistic. She can do anything she sets her mind to, really. She knits and paints. She's played around with designing jewelry. A very talented young lady, if I do say so myself."

"Would she have told anyone your secret?"

"She's very quiet," Diane said. "I can't imagine she would do that. When she was little, I could hardly get her to speak at all. She'd even hide behind me whenever someone would talk to her. She's not one to speak up. I worry about her sometimes."

"Then how did someone find out?"

Diane shook her head. "I have no idea. No idea. We do the work here at my house. I haven't told anyone else."

"Do you mind if I talk to her?" Shannon waited, hoping for an affirmative response.

"You're such a nice young lady. You won't scare her, will you? The girl is as jumpy as a Mexican bean sometimes. I'd hate to frighten her." Diane twisted her hands together again.

Shannon touched Diane's arm. "I won't scare her. I promise."

Diane grabbed another sheet of paper and scribbled something on it. "Here you go. Please, be kind. She means the world to me."

"I will. Thank you."

A few minutes later, Shannon stepped out the door and glanced at the name and address on the paper.

*Laura Applebee.*

# — 17 —

Shannon entered Laura's address into her GPS. The girl didn't live far away—about halfway between her grandmother's house and Apple Grove. Shannon decided to swing past the girl's apartment building since she was already in the area.

She'd wanted to ask Diane to see a picture of the girl, but she didn't want to upset the woman by suggesting that her granddaughter may have been behind any of the recent mayhem.

What if Laura Applebee had assumed that Sunny was the one behind the blackmail notes sent to Diane? What if she'd wanted to eliminate anyone who threatened her grandmother?

Shannon pulled into the parking lot of an older apartment complex. She checked the address one more time before climbing out of her truck and starting toward the wooden stairs.

What would Michael say if he knew she was doing this? He wouldn't be very happy, especially since he'd appointed himself her personal guardian. She *could* potentially be confronting a killer.

Shannon's cellphone was in her purse, and she had Michael on speed dial. She'd use it if she ran into trouble.

Doubt began gathering like a storm in her mind. Perhaps confronting Laura alone wasn't such a good idea. But she refused to turn back now. She needed answers. Thoughts about Rupert Murphy, her shop, the Purls, her mother and children, Michael and Hunter swirled through her mind.

Shannon shook her head. She had to concentrate on the task at hand.

She climbed the steps that led to the second level of the apartment building. Four doors waited for her there. She found number 41B and knocked.

Her throat went dry as she waited. What would happen when Laura answered? Would things turn ugly?

A chill brushed over her as the wind swept through the enclave.

She knocked again.

Still no answer.

"I don't think Laura is home," someone said behind her. "Her car's not out front."

She gasped and turned to find a tall, college-age boy standing right behind her.

He grinned. "Didn't mean to scare you."

"I guess I was so lost in thought that I didn't hear you," she said. "Do you know Laura?"

He shrugged. "About as well as anyone does, which isn't very well. She keeps to herself. Even if she is home, sometimes she doesn't answer the door. Depends on if she's deep into one of her projects or not."

"Projects?"

"Yeah, she's all about art. She's always working on something. She's pretty good. Not that I know anything about art. Anyway, she's been coming and going a lot lately. Not sure what's going on."

"Maybe you could help me. I'm not sure I have the right person. Is Laura petite with light brown hair?"

He nodded. "Yeah, and she kind of walks with her shoulders

drooped. You think *I'm* quiet? She could sneak up on any-one. She's that quiet."

Shannon nodded. Laura was definitely the girl who'd come into the craft market to buy stained glass art supplies. She was probably the same person who'd been leaving her notes. And she may have murdered Sunny Davis. Shannon felt certain Laura was connected with all of it. "Thank you for your help."

"No problem."

Shannon hurried back to her truck. She had to call Michael and tell him the news.

*　　　*　　　*

Shannon pushed END on her phone before sliding the device into her purse and cranking the engine. No surprise, Michael had urged her to call Grayson and let him handle tracking down Laura. Michael had reminded her that Laura could be "off her rocker." After all, *someone* had shot at him, poisoned Sunny, and left lead dust in Shannon's drink. If that person indeed was Laura Applebee, Shannon needed to keep her distance.

Shannon had to agree. She was unarmed and untrained—and she'd actually agreed to call Grayson and leave the investigation to him.

Michael was thrilled when Shannon acquiesced—thrilled and clearly shocked. Shannon chuckled, remembering his slight stammer on the phone. She'd told him that she had to stop by Alana's to drop off the scarf, but that she'd swing by his office on her way back into town.

She checked her voicemail and saw that Erica had called. She must have gotten special permission from the police to place a call from jail. Shannon was eager to tell her the news. But first, she'd wait for the police to pick up Laura for questioning.

With a sigh, she put the truck in gear and slowly drove down the hill. With any luck, the nightmare would come to an end soon. Relief started to soften her tight muscles. She could resume her life again and move on to the other issues at hand—things like Rupert's job offer.

As she drove, she mulled over the twisted road that had been her investigation. Everyone seemed to have deep, dark secrets of some kind. Diane was being blackmailed. Mark Arnold's shows were losing traction and making him desperate. James Knight had been dating Sunny. But those secrets were just that—secrets. Not motives or reasons to murder.

Could it be this simple? Had desperation to protect her grandmother provoked Laura to do such a terrible thing? Was that mousy, frail girl a cold-blooded killer? If so, why in the world had she left Shannon the notes—or had those come from someone else? Shannon hoped she'd discover the answers to those questions once the girl was interrogated.

Shannon gripped the steering wheel tightly as Old Blue bounced down the road. One day, the old truck was going to leave her stranded. Until then, she'd continue to drive it as a way of honoring her heritage. Though she'd never met her grandparents, she liked to imagine each of them sitting in the driver's seat, their hands touching the same wheel and controls.

Ten minutes later, she pulled into Alana's driveway. She grabbed her purse, checking quickly to make sure the scarf was still inside.

Shannon hadn't told Alana she was coming, but she hoped the woman was home. If not, she'd try to tuck the accessory into the door handle or somewhere where the wind and rain wouldn't catch it.

Shannon knocked on the door and waited. Just as she raised her fist to knock again, Alana pulled it open and greeted her with a smile.

"Shannon, what a nice surprise," she said.

Shannon held up the scarf. "I found this after you left the funeral yesterday."

Alana waved her hand in the air as if embarrassed. "I was wondering what happened to that old thing. I appreciate you driving all the way out here."

"It's no problem. I had to take a trip this way anyway."

"Why don't you come in out of the cold for a moment? You'll catch your death in this weather."

"Oh, I don't want to impose."

"You're not. Come in and visit for a minute—I insist."

Shannon smiled. Visiting for a second wouldn't hurt. Michael had told her he planned to work in his office all afternoon, so she didn't have to worry about missing him. She stepped inside and let the heat envelop her as Alana closed the door.

Alana pointed to the table in the distance. "Have a seat, make yourself comfortable. I was just about to warm up some water for tea. Would you like a cup?"

Shannon started to refuse but stopped herself. Hot tea

sounded wonderful, and she could finally drink tea again without fear of being poisoned. "I'd love some."

Alana disappeared into the kitchen. Shannon heard sounds of a teakettle being filled and placed on the stove in the other room. A moment later, Alana reappeared and sat across from her.

"It will be ready soon." Alana sat back for a moment and her eyebrow quirked. "So you were up in this neck of the woods? Not many people take visits up here."

"I was checking on a friend."

"Let me guess—Diane Sigmund."

"How'd you know?" Shannon nodded, impressed.

Alana smiled. "The art world can be a small one, especially when you've been around it for as long as I have. Diane and I have done shows together in the past. She's a very talented lady—probably one of the best in her art form."

Shannon nodded. "I agree. Her work is fantastic." Not entirely "hers" anymore—but nonetheless, Shannon would never divulge Diane's secret.

"I admire that lady. Even with her arthritis, she keeps going. The amount of pain she must be in to create one of those balls? I can't imagine it." Alana shook her head. "I don't know if I would be that dedicated."

"I'm not sure if I would be either." Shannon knew she should drop the subject, but curiosity got the best of her. "Yesterday at the funeral, you said you suspected one of your students may have had something to do with Sunny's death."

Alana nodded and smoothed out the place mat in front of her. "Yes. Laura Applebee."

"Tell me again why you suspect her of being involved."

The woman shrugged and folded her fingers together. "I don't anymore. Last night I heard that someone had been arrested for Sunny's death, so I guess it was my overactive imagination projecting onto the poor girl."

"But it seemed like you might have had more to tell me. I'd like to hear it."

The kettle whistled. "Hold that thought." Alana disappeared into the kitchen and returned a moment later with two cups of steaming tea.

Shannon took her first sip. "This is strong."

Alana nodded. "It's a brand I buy at a market in Portland. All organic. It's supposed to be good for your immune system. It's my secret for staying young." She winked and took a sip.

Shannon raised her cup again, but stopped and said, "This time of the year, you can't boost your immune system too much, can you?"

"Not at all. Especially when you get to be my age. I'm not as strong as I once was. You need every little extra boost you can get." Alana let out a brittle laugh before coughing. "Maybe I need to start drinking more. Listen to that hack. It always happens at this time of the year."

Shannon leaned back in her chair, still mulling over Sunny's death. She'd told Michael she would back off, and only a few minutes ago, she'd been patting herself on the back for agreeing to do just that. But asking a few more questions couldn't hurt anything ... could it? "Tell me about Laura."

Alana nodded quickly. "Right, right. I'd nearly forgotten." She paused, tapping her nail against the side of her cup. "Now that I think about it, you may have met Laura at the art show last week. I talked her into volunteering there. The guild was desperate for people to help."

"Laura was there?" Shannon searched her memory but couldn't place her.

Alana nodded. "She helped hand out water bottles."

Shannon blinked. Of course—that's why the girl had looked so familiar. "The water girl."

Alana waved her hand in the air. "I know what you're thinking. That would be too easy, right? But indeed, the girl was there. Of course, she disappeared after Sunny died. That's what first raised my suspicions about her. When I heard that Sunny had been poisoned, and that they'd found some kind of drug in her water bottle, that's when I *really* got suspicious."

"But based on what you told me at the funeral, you were suspicious before the art show—correct?"

Alana's eyebrows shot upward. "Laura's a strange one. Very talented. She can do anything she sets her mind to. But she's so quiet and brooding that you never quite know what she's thinking. You know what I mean?"

Shannon nodded. "I do." She'd found the girl to be a bit strange also.

"Her lessons here were generally held right before Sunny arrived for our weekly chats, so they crossed paths sometimes. I think she really admired Sunny's work. She may have even resented Sunny for being so talented. I don't know. I couldn't get a good read on the girl."

Shannon took another sip of her tea. "Do you think she was capable of murder?"

Alana snorted. "I don't know if I'd say that. Being

strange doesn't mean you're a murderer, does it? Besides, what motive would the girl have?"

Shannon shook her head, confused by Alana's change of tune. "You tell me."

Alana shrugged. "I have no idea. Before Erica was arrested, I thought Laura might be someone you should check out. Now that Erica is behind bars, I suppose there's no need. I doubt I'll ever see the girl around here again. She's probably gone for good."

Shannon leaned back in her chair, suddenly tired. Was it the rain? The drive? The thought of all the responsibilities waiting for her back in Apple Grove?

She wasn't sure.

That's when she saw Alana smirk from across the table.

What a strange expression. The woman almost seemed ... satisfied? Like that cat who ate the canary, as the saying went.

As Shannon's thinking continued to cloud, realization slowly washed over her.

Laura Applebee wasn't the killer at all.

Alana Golden was the mastermind behind it all.

# — 18 —

Shannon could tell by the look in Alana's eyes that the woman was twisted.

She also knew from the way the room seemed to be spinning that she didn't have much time before she'd be unable to defend herself.

Her purse was in her lap under the table. Casually, she reached into it, found her cellphone, located the "2" key and held it down.

*Michael. With any luck, he'll answer the phone and overhear the conversation.*

Shannon's eyelids began to droop.

She prayed that he would answer his phone. She'd told him she was dropping the scarf off at Alana's. Would he put everything together? She prayed he would. He was her only hope.

Alana's smirk morphed into a broad grin, and she leaned across the table toward Shannon. "Are you feeling OK? You're looking pale. Do you need to lie down?"

"No. Must be the weather," Shannon mumbled. Her words were becoming slurred, and her brain seemed like mush.

"Are you sure you don't want to lie down?"

Shannon shook her head, but she was unsure how long she'd be able to remain upright. What exactly had the woman put in her tea? Cyanide? Shannon picked up her purse and tried to stand. Her legs wouldn't hold her, and she sank back into her seat. "No, I should be going."

"It's not good to drive if you're feeling lightheaded, dear."

Shannon didn't have much time, nor did she have anything to lose. She stared at Alana, trying to keep her thoughts focused. "Why'd you do it?"

Alana raised an eyebrow. "Do what?"

"Why'd you kill Sunny and try to frame poor Laura Applebee and Erica Winters?"

The woman's smile widened. Did she have no mercy? Did she delight in what she'd done? Alana stood and began pacing around the room. "Someone had to be framed. *I* certainly didn't want to go to jail for her death."

Shannon ran her hand over her phone. If only she could know for sure that her plan had worked—that Michael had answered and heard what was happening so he could get help. If he hadn't answered ... Well, she was going to die. Perhaps she should have called 9-1-1 instead. She wasn't thinking clearly. She felt her phone slide off her lap. "Why? Why Sunny?"

Alana's smile disappeared, and she paused from her pacing. "Do you know how hard it is when your student becomes better than you are?" The woman put her hand on her hip, looking as casual as most people did when they talked about something mundane like grocery shopping. "Sunny's work was effortless, and she made more money than she knew what to do with. People begged her to be in their shows. She got so much work that she had to turn people away."

The room was no longer spinning—it was starting to whirl with sharp horizon shifts. Shannon felt her stomach roil. Things couldn't end this way. She had so much she needed to do—and all of it involved her family and friends. Life came into absolute and complete clarity. She clung to the edge of the table, trying to focus on Alana. "So you murdered her?"

Alana glanced at her fingernails and played with a chip in her polish for a moment. "Without Sunny in the picture, I can get more work. I've already had three people call me this week about doing jobs that Sunny was supposed to do. Isn't that wonderful?"

"I thought you said your husband left you enough money to live on."

"Don't always believe everything people tell you, darling. My husband lost all of our money in one big, bad business venture. The one thing he *did* leave me was some cyanide from his old textile company. Textile companies use cyanide to make their fabrics. The chemical is harder than you think to get your hands on, you know."

"No, I don't know."

"I tried poisoning Sunny's tea with a little lead. I have this wonderful old pot that is just full of contaminates. It makes wonderful tea; it's so sweet—but that method of poisoning was taking entirely too long. That's when I added a smidge of cyanide to a bottle of water. I switched the bottles out at the show to make sure she got the right one."

Shannon shook her head, but the motion only made her field of vision worse. She'd had no idea how twisted the woman was. "You blackmailed Diane Sigmund to make sure there was an opening in the show, didn't you? But there were no guarantees that you'd get her slot and not someone else."

Alana looked up from examining her nails and sneered. "Sunny put in a good word for me. Mark Arnold always did whatever Sunny asked. He was practically like a little puppy dog around her. He knew that without Sunny at his shows, he wouldn't get the same clientele as when she was there."

"Why would Sunny want you at the show?" Shannon felt her body start to slump. How much longer did she have before she lost consciousness? Before her body went into shock and death claimed her? If only she could stand.

"Because I threatened to tell everyone that she was dating James Knight if she didn't."

Alana morphed into two people as Shannon's vision doubled. Still, she managed to mutter, "What did that matter? People date all the time."

"Because James was in a relationship with someone else when they started dating, that's why. It would have ruined Sunny's squeaky-clean reputation. Come on—all the stained glass work she does for churches. Do you really think they're going to want to work with someone who breaks up relationships? Word spreads about these things, you know."

"You thought of everything, didn't you?"

Alana's smile returned. "Of course. Thinking of everything is what I do best. If the evidence I planted implicating Erica Winters falls through, I've set up sufficient evidence to make it look like Laura Applebee was losing her mind and acting in psychotic ways. I even found some ridiculous notes that Laura left for Sunny. That girl is always leaving notes. Doesn't she know she should never put certain things in writing?"

"You're not going to get away with this." Shannon's ears began to ring, and all she could hear was that and Alana's twisted laughter echoing throughout the room. She braced her hands on the table, her palms spread out against the wood, and used every bit of her willpower to stand.

"We'll see about that, dear."

Shannon had to do something, but her body wasn't cooperating. All she could do was stand while clinging to the table—and she could barely do that. "What did you poison me with?"

"Cyanide, of course. But that won't be the official cause of your death. There will be a tragic accident on your way to see me. Your truck will go off the side of one of the treacherous roads around here. Really, what were you thinking, driving that truck? It's a piece of junk and not very safe at all." Alana paused. "Your family and friends will be so devastated when they find out what happened. They'll probably blame themselves for not insisting you get a more reliable vehicle."

"There are other ways to get help financially besides murder, you know. You didn't have to kill someone to get ahead."

"You don't know what desperate is, dear." Alana's voice turned bitter. "You don't know what it's like to see your dreams slip through your fingers. I gave up everything for my husband's career. My stained glass was all I had, and Sunny was taking all of my business. Can you believe that?"

"There's room for more than one stained glass artist in the world."

"I've never been good at being second best." Alana approached Shannon and lifted the teacup to Shannon's mouth. "Why don't you drink a little more and hasten this process? I have a hair appointment soon."

Shannon managed to muster enough energy to swat the drink away. The cup flew through the air and crashed on the floor. Liquid stained the wooden planks at their feet and splashed onto the curtain.

*Good. Maybe the police will detect cyanide there.*

"You silly girl. Didn't your mother ever teach you any manners?" Alana asked. "Not to worry, I will just pour you another cup."

Shannon's mother never taught her anything. But her mouth wouldn't move to say so. Blackness was closing in.

*Please, Michael. Get here. Call the police. Help me.*

Just as the blackness began to overwhelm her, someone burst through the front door.

Only, it wasn't Michael.

It was Laura Applebee.

*       *       *

Shannon dropped to the floor. It was becoming increasingly difficult to move. The cyanide had begun to paralyze her, to take away movement. To take away logic.

To take away life.

But through the haze, she could see Laura point a gun at Alana. The sick, twisted smile finally disappeared from the woman's face, replaced by fear.

Alana paced in an arch around Laura. "Now, now, Laura. You don't have to come unglued over this. We can work something out here."

"You were blackmailing my grandmother!" she yelled. The gun shook in her hands as she stepped toward Alana. "Why would you do that?"

"I can't believe you have to ask." Alana snapped. *"You're* the one who told me you were helping her with the Temari balls."

The girl's eyes bulged. *"Helping.* I said I was helping!"

Alana flicked a piece of lint from her sweater. "It was easy to piece together that you were doing most of the work, dear. Your grandmother can hardly hold a fork. There's no way she could hold a needle. She should give it up."

The gun still trembled in Laura's fingers, but she showed no sign of backing down. "She has bills to pay too, you know. My granddad died of cancer. His medical bills took all of our money. Then *you* tried to take everything else."

Shannon fought to remain lucid, to retain a hold on her consciousness. Had Michael heard any of this? If he had, would he get here in time?

"The police will discover your fingerprints on the water bottle, Laura. I suggest you get out of here now. Otherwise, I'll plant more evidence to make it look like you tampered with Shannon's truck."

"I'm not afraid of you. Not anymore." Laura straightened her elbows and her index finger flexed over the trigger.

Lying on the floor near Alana, Shannon thought of the people in her life she cared for. Lara, Alec, Beth, Deborah, the Purls, her best friend in Scotland, Coleen ... all of their faces paraded through her mind. Even Michael's—he'd warned her to stay out of this.

"You're not afraid?" Alana resumed pacing in a semicircle in front of Laura. "You should be. I've mastered the art of manipulating people. It was the only way I could get the collectors off my back. My husband taught me everything I know. He said manipulation was the only way to succeed in business."

"Your husband was wrong," Shannon mumbled. "Having integrity earns you success ... and ... respect."

Alana shoved Shannon with her foot. "Still hanging on, are you? I should have upped the dose in your tea. I'll know better next time." She leaned down and pursed her lips at Shannon. "Soon all of this agony will be over. I do hope you wrote a will, so someone will get that nice house and business of yours."

Shannon tried to reach forward, desperate to grab the woman and shake her. But her limbs wouldn't cooperate. Instead, she settled for scowling at the woman from the floor. Her vision faded in and out. It blurred, doubled, and then cleared for a moment.

Laura looked at Shannon. "I tried to tell you, Mrs. McClain."

*Why didn't you?* Shannon wanted to ask. But she knew. Laura hadn't wanted to implicate her grandmother. By telling everything she knew, she would have exposed Diane. Instead she'd left the notes in hopes that Shannon would track down the bad guy—in this case, Alana.

Shannon wasn't sure why Laura had chosen to engage her in solving the crime. And now she doubted she'd live long enough to find out.

Based on the pain that radiated through her, the end must be near.

She hoped that Alec and Lara knew how much she loved them.

And the Purls. They'd become like family to her.

The whole town of Apple Grove, for that matter. They'd filled so many voids in her life. There had been times after John had died that she didn't know how she was going to survive. Then she'd been blessed with a fresh start in Oregon.

Shannon wasn't sure if she was hallucinating or not

when she saw Alana swing her leg around and kick the gun from Laura's hands.

Someone screamed.

A gun fired.

Then a familiar figure rushed into the room.

*Michael.* He'd come.

But was he too late?

Shannon feared the worst as the blackness overtook her completely.

# — 19 —

Shannon pulled her eyes open.

Beeps, glaring lights, sterile white walls.

She must be in the hospital.

Or was it the morgue?

The entire fiasco at Alana's flooded into her mind. She'd been poisoned. Then Laura had come. Alana had knocked the gun from her hands, and Michael had stormed inside.

There was a shot. Was he OK? What about Laura? *Where is Alana now?*

Her gaze focused on the room around her. Not the morgue. It was definitely the hospital. She'd survived the whole, terrible ordeal.

Tears rushed to her eyes at the thought of everything. She'd come so close to leaving this world. There was still so much she wanted to do. So much she wanted to say. She wasn't ready to go yet.

"Mum! Are you OK?" Lara rushed to her bedside. Tears gleamed in her eyes.

Alec appeared on the other side of her bed. "You gave us a good scare."

Shannon took Lara's hand on one side of her, and Alec's on the other. She squeezed—probably harder than she should have. "I've never been so happy to see you two."

"We're happy to see you awake," Alec said. "We came

right away. Michael called and told us you'd been poisoned."

Her mother, Beth, stepped from behind the twins and ran a hand across Shannon's forehead. "So glad you're OK, honey. That was too close."

"There are other people here to see you too," Lara said, nodding toward the door.

Shannon smiled. "Let me guess—the Purls?"

"Yes, of course the Purls are here. But there are a couple of others, as well. They've all been camping out in the waiting room."

Shannon tried to pull herself up, but the effort expended too much energy. She settled instead on pushing her head back into the pillow. "How long have I been here?"

"About nine hours." Alec looked over his shoulder. "I'm going to tell the doctor you're awake. I'm sure he'll want to see you."

A moment later, an older man in a white coat came into the room. "Glad to see you're still with us, Mrs. McClain. I'm Dr. Stevens."

She licked her dry lips. "I'm glad too. And surprised, quite frankly. I thought the cyanide had irreversibly taken hold."

"It almost did," Dr. Stevens said, his expression grim. "We started you on drugs to counteract the poison the moment you arrived. We caught it in the nick of time. Thirty minutes longer and it might have been too late."

Shannon shuddered at the thought. That had been close. Too close.

The doctor patted her hand. "It looks like you're going to be fine. We plan to keep you here for another day or two, to make sure. You might feel weak, but you'll rebuild your strength with time."

Shannon nodded. "I understand. Thank you for everything."

The doctor pointed toward the door. "There's a man in the hallway who'd like to speak with you. Is it all right if I send him in?"

"A police officer?"

He shrugged. "I didn't see a badge."

Hunter? She owed him an apology for doubting his story and suspecting that he was somehow involved in Sunny's murder. She nodded to the doctor. "Yes, please do."

But it was Michael who stepped into the room. He handed her a wildflower bouquet. "To help you get better soon."

Taken aback, she pulled them under her nose and inhaled the sweet scent. He'd never given her flowers before. "They're beautiful, Michael. Thank you."

"Well, I couldn't let Hunter show me up too much, now could I?" His eyes twinkled.

She didn't know what to say to that, so she remained quiet. She wasn't sure she'd ever figure Michael out. Maybe it was better that way—better for her heart, at least.

"What happened?" She rested the flowers on her chest. "The last thing I remember was hearing a gunshot, and then seeing you burst in."

He stood at her bedside, his hands resting on the railing as he looked at her. His eyes were warm. "Alana and Laura got into a struggle. The gun fired, but no one was hit, fortunately. The police have enough evidence to put Alana away for a long, long time."

"Thank goodness. That woman should never be allowed

to roam free among the rest of society again. She's crazy, and she's ruined too many lives. To think, she almost got away with murder."

Michael nodded.

"I assume you got my phone call?" Shannon asked. "Is that how you knew where to go?"

"I got your call, and I heard what was taking place in the background. Fortunately, I was already on my way to Alana's."

She blinked in surprise. "Why?"

"When you said Alana's name, something clicked in my head. Her name sounded familiar. When I worked as a detective in Portland, we investigated the death of her spouse."

Shannon felt her jaw drop. "She killed her husband?"

"We never found enough evidence to arrest her, but we always suspected she had a hand in his death. The case may be reopened now that this new information has emerged. I suspect she may have slipped something into his drink also. After all, he owned a textile company that used cyanide in its processes."

"I can't believe it. As crazy as she is, it never occurred to me that she might have killed her husband."

"I was trying to catch you before you got to her house, but apparently you turned your ringer off."

Shannon realized she'd turned her ringer off at Sunny's funeral. She'd never remembered to turn it back on. "Lucky for me you decided to dig a little deeper. I wouldn't be here if you hadn't." She smiled at him. "As I've told you before, you have a knack for finding me at just the right moment."

Michael stared into her eyes for a moment. He opened his mouth as if he might say something but then closed it again. He stepped away and asked, "Do you mind if I bring someone else in for a moment? She's been rather anxious to speak with you."

*Who could it be?* Shannon nodded, more curious than ever. "Not at all."

He went to the door and motioned at someone to come in.

Laura stepped inside. The girl looked at Shannon and then quickly glanced at the floor, her timidity peeking through again. She paused several feet from the bed and rubbed her hands together.

"You certainly didn't look this timid when you burst through the door at Alana's house," Shannon said with a smile. She nodded at Michael, who lingered in the background, and he let the two of them have their moment uninterrupted. "You helped to save my life."

Laura looked up and offered a shy smile. But she didn't speak.

"One question, Laura. I assume it was you who left me those notes. Why me?"

Laura took another tentative step closer. "I like to get my cupcakes at Pink Sprinkles. They have the best pastries around. I overheard some customers and one of the ladies at the store mention how you'd helped to solve some crimes in Apple Grove. I knew you were the only person who could help, just like I knew that Alana had killed Sunny."

"How did you know Alana was guilty?"

"I stopped by to pick up some of my supplies last week, and I saw her messing with a water bottle—the exact kind of water that Sunny drank. I only knew because I'd read an article on Sunny where she talked about her quirky habits. Anyway, Alana didn't hear me there, but I knew what she was doing. I volunteered to help at the show. I wanted to make sure Sunny didn't get one of those bottles. I guess I was too late."

"But what made you suspect that Alana wanted to kill Sunny in the first place?"

Laura shrugged. "It was obvious, and Alana wasn't good at hiding her true feelings around me. I'm a detail person. I pay attention to everything—including how concerned you were with everyone." She took another step closer. "I knew you could find the answers, Mrs. McClain, and prove that I was right. Thank you."

Warmth spread through Shannon. As much as she wished the girl had just gone straight to the police with her suspicions about Alana, based on what her grandmother had said about her, Shannon understood why Laura hadn't.

"There's even better news, Laura."

The girl blinked. "What's that?"

"I got a voicemail yesterday from Erica Winters. She'd set a reward for whoever solved Sunny's murder. I think you and your grandmother should get that money."

Laura's eyes widened. "You really think so? I know that would help her so much!"

Shannon nodded. "Yeah, I really think so. Hopefully she can pay off some of those medical bills."

Laura threw her arms around Shannon, but quickly pulled back and glanced at Michael. "Sorry for shooting at you."

His eyes widened before narrowing into a scowl. "That was you?"

She nodded. "I wasn't trying to hit you. I just didn't want you to figure out who I was. I was afraid for—" She glanced at Shannon.

Shannon raised a hand, trying to let Laura know that she didn't have to finish. The girl was afraid for her grandmother. Shannon knew what it was like to protect those who were close to you.

Shannon squeezed the girl's hand. "Thank you for everything, Laura. I appreciate your help. And your notes. They kept me going."

Laura nodded.

"I hear you're an amazing artist," Shannon continued. "I'd love to see your work sometime."

A hint of a smile stretched across Laura's face. "Maybe I'll bring something by the Paisley Craft Market."

"That would be wonderful. I have a loft space open— you might want to think about renting one."

Laura nodded again. "I will. Thank you, Mrs. McClain. You're a real lifesaver." She said her goodbyes and left the room.

Michael smiled at Shannon. "You're going to send me to my grave early. You know that, don't you?"

"I'm sorry, Michael."

He shook his head "Don't be sorry. Your investigation has helped a lot of people. Speaking of which," he nodded toward the door, "all the Purls are desperate to see you. Mind if I send them in?"

"Please do."

His head swung toward the door again. "I think I'm going to take off and see if Grayson needs my help with anything. You going to be OK here?"

Shannon nodded. "Of course. It looks like I'll be in here for a day or two. I'll call you when I'm released from the hospital."

"I'm only a phone call away."

"You probably noticed it already, but you're on my speed dial." She didn't mention that he'd been there for quite a while.

"Good. Keep me there." He left with a nod. Then, like a dam bursting, her friends flooded into the room and surrounded her bed.

Joyce pulled out a bedazzled hospital gown. "I made it just in case, you know," she said with a small grin.

Shannon laughed. "Just in case I almost got myself killed again?"

"I was sort of playing with the idea in general," Joyce said. "You get to be my test project."

"It's beautiful. Thank you." Shannon touched the standard hospital garb, which now had a line of fuchsia stones gracing the collar line. "I think I know what our next charity project should be. What a way to brighten someone's hospital visit."

"The doctor said we can't stay long," Betty said. "But we wanted to drop by. We were so worried. Michael called all of us."

"And we have something for you," Melanie said, handing Shannon a ribbon.

"What's this?"

"It's an award for Most Curious in Show. We thought you rightfully earned it," Melanie explained.

"I guess that's better than one for Deadliest in Show," Shannon replied.

Everyone laughed.

*Friends and family.* Those were the important things in life, Shannon realized as they fussed and clacked over her.

# — 20 —

"Watch your step." Michael pointed at one of the cobblestones leading to Shannon's front door.

"I was poisoned, not maimed," Shannon insisted.

The doctor had finally released her from the hospital on Monday evening after keeping her there for two days of observation. She'd never been so happy to be home.

Michael held her elbow as he walked her to the front door. He'd been attentive and the perfect gentleman ever since he'd rescued her from Alana's house—not that he ever *wasn't* the perfect gentleman. Still, his friendship meant a lot.

She turned toward him on the stoop. "I'm fine. Really. You didn't have to go through all of this trouble."

He shrugged. "I know, but I wanted to. The Purls arranged for Joyce to pick up Old Blue for you, so you had to have a ride home from the hospital."

She looked up at Michael, noticing how the soft porch light illuminated his face and eyes. "Would you like tea?" She gulped as she said the words. Tea had gotten her into too much trouble, it seemed. "Better yet, how about some coffee?"

He grinned. "That sounds good, but only if you let me fix it."

"It's a deal." She shoved her key into the lock and pushed the door open. At once, a chorus of "Surprise!" rang out from the inside.

Shannon felt her mouth drop open in shock. Her eyes

swept the crowd, and she spotted all of her dearest friends and family, including her mom. She finally found her voice and exclaimed, "Och! What are you all doing here? It's not my birthday. I'm sorry to break it to you."

Melanie stepped forward. "We know. But we thought we'd surprise you and let you know how special you are to us. We were awfully close to losing you the other day."

"You're not getting rid of me that easily," Shannon teased. "I'm a hardy Scottish lass, you know."

A chorus of laughter scattered through the room. Shannon wandered from person to person, catching up briefly with each one. Michael thrust a mug of coffee into her hands, and she took a long sip, thankful for the dose of caffeine.

She was surprised to see several unexpected faces there also. Laura had shown up with her grandmother, Diane. Even James and Mark had made appearances.

As she was talking to the twins and her mother, a heavy hand came down on her shoulder. She twirled in time to see Hunter standing there. "Hey, beautiful. You had me worried. You doing OK?"

She nodded and waved to Lara, Alec, and her mom, who went on to mingle. "Never been better."

He gave her a boyish grin. "I'm glad to hear that. I'm sorry that I haven't been able to see you sooner. I was stuck out on a boat doing a field study that required my presence. I've been out of the loop."

"That's all right. I'm glad this is all cleared up." Shannon sighed. "To think that I even suspected *you* for awhile."

His eyebrows shot up. "You suspected *me*?"

She waved her hand in the air. "I heard a rumor that the

company you work for doesn't really exist. It made me overly suspicious at the time."

His eyes clouded for a moment. "Someone told you that?"

"Isn't it crazy? My conspiracy theories began to get the best of me, and I apologize."

His trademark grin returned. "I can see how that might happen with everything that's going on. I can assure you, the company I work for might be new, but it's real."

*It's a new business ... mystery solved. Perhaps Michael's research skills are slipping a bit.*

Hunter nodded behind her. "It looks like there's a line of people waiting to talk to you. I don't want to keep you from the party."

"Thanks, Hunter. Maybe we could get coffee again sometime."

His grin widened. "I would really like that."

Shannon turned and found herself face-to-face with Erica. The woman threw her arms around Shannon. "Thank you for everything, Shannon. I don't know where I'd be without you."

"I'd like to think that the truth would have come out somehow."

"Sure, maybe after I'd wasted years in jail. Maybe never." Erica shivered. "I don't like thinking about it."

Shannon took her arm and led her to a corner. "Listen, there's something I wanted to tell you. I was talking to the doctor while I was in the hospital. He told me something pretty interesting about lead poisoning."

"What's that?"

"He said that when a person has been exposed to lead, that it can change their personality. It can make a person more irritable and more easily angered." Shannon lowered her voice. "I know that you and Sunny didn't get along all that well over the last few months. I wanted to let you know that some of Sunny's actions may have been brought on by lead exposure."

Erica threw her arms around Shannon again. "That's so good to hear! Our friendship had become so strained; I couldn't seem to do anything right around her. I hated that."

"It might explain why she broke up with James also."

Erica's jaw dropped open. "*James Knight?* She and James were dating?" She shook her head. "I should have realized it. I saw the way they looked at each other, but I assumed the fire in their eyes was part of their competitive natures. They were both used to being celebrated artists. Now that I think about it, they would have been perfect together."

"Sometimes heightened feelings can seem negative when they're really quite the opposite. People who may appear to dislike each other might actually be fighting feelings that are anything *but* dislike."

"Is that right?"

She looked up to see Michael had rejoined her. She hardly wanted to acknowledge the fact that her heart skipped a beat at the sight of him. And now her words came back to haunt her. Sometimes she and Michael appeared to be fire and ice. Was that because, in truth, their feelings actually ran deeper?

"I don't mean to interrupt, but the Purls have something they want to show you." He nodded across the foyer.

"Oh? Then I'd better get over there." Shannon excused herself as Michael led her away. The Purls waited in the kitchen. They all huddled together with big grins on their faces.

"I wanted to show you this," Joyce said, stepping forward and thrusting something toward her. "It's the article about you from *The Artist's Touch*. We printed it right from the website so we could show you. It's wonderful," Betty said.

Her vision finally cleared, and she saw her face right below the nameplate for *The Artist's Touch*. "When Roberta said 'feature story,' I had no idea I would be the *cover* story." Shannon took the pages from Joyce.

"It's a lovely picture," Melanie said. "It shows how beautiful you are."

"As does the article," Kate said. "You should check it out."

Shannon's gaze roamed over her friends for a moment before she flipped through the papers, first looking at the pictures of her with her jewelry and in her store.

She read the words, and her cheeks flushed. The article was wonderful, filled with lots of compliments. She dismissed the hype with a wave as she looked up. "I don't know where the reporter came up with all of this. It's blarney, pure and simple."

Essie put her hand on her shoulder. "It's the truth. You're one of the most giving people I know. I'm glad the reporter chose to highlight that, along with your other accomplishments."

"I'd say you're well on your way, with or without that offer from Rupert," Betty said.

Shannon swallowed hard. "I called him from the hospital."

The mood in the room turned tense.

"Did you?" Joyce said. "And?"

"And I told him I was flattered, but very content with my life here in Apple Grove." A round of applause rose around her.

Joyce wrapped her arms around Shannon and said, "We're glad you're not leaving us. You have no idea. But I'm sorry you'll miss this opportunity. It was going to be big."

"When life is over, it's not how much money you made or how high you climbed on the ladder of success that will matter. It's the people whose lives you've touched and those who have touched you."

"I'd say you've touched a lot of lives," Melanie said. "I know you've touched mine."

"And mine," Erica said from the doorway.

Standing behind Erica, Mark rolled his eyes. "I suppose you've even touched mine, though I hate to admit it."

Shannon laughed and felt tears of joy escape her eyes. "You're all wonderful. Thank you for everything."

The Purls closed in around her in a group hug. No, she wouldn't trade her life in Apple Grove for anything.

Learn more about Annie's fiction books at

# AnniesFiction.com

- Access your e-books
- Discover exciting new series
- Read sample chapters
- Watch video book trailers
- Share your feedback

---

## We've designed the Annie's Fiction website especially for you!

---

## Plus, manage your account online!

- Check your account status
- Make payments online
- Update your address

Visit us at AnniesFiction.com

Enjoy this exclusive preview
of the next mystery in the
Creative Woman Mysteries series.

# Guilty Treasures

**COMING SOON!**

# — Prologue —

Oregon Coast, February 1942

"**I**t's gold." Captain James Paisley stroked the coin's surface. His fingers tingled as they outlined the worn cross and lion stamped into tarnished metal. He'd spent months of wracking his brain, endlessly searching in the dark by flashlight, sometimes digging like a mole during the sea's cold, angry months—the only time when frolickers deserted the beach—but it couldn't steal the warmth pumping through him.

"Spanish doubloon, Cap'n?" His first mate's young eyes gleamed. Corny stretched a finger to touch the coin.

James squelched the urge to yank it away. "The real thing. Right era—late sixteenth century."

"How much is it worth?"

"Think I'd tell you?" James forced a smile and handed the doubloon to Corny.

The kid caressed it like the face of a long-lost love.

"OK, enough," James said. "After all that work, we'd better stick it someplace safe before we lose it."

"I'll keep it for you." Grinning, Corny pretended to pocket the doubloon.

James chuckled as he snatched the coin and deposited it

inside his coat. "After we're done, I'll buy you a hot-buttered rum. We can sit by a fire and admire the coin all night."

"Sounds great." Corny's smirk widened. "Even better if you keep the drinks comin', Cap'n."

"Count on it," James said, though even the best tavern euphoria couldn't match his sense of accomplishment right now. The shoreline crags had tried to hide Parable Rock, the crosslike formation, from him. His ancestor Angus Paisley had taunted him with cryptic clues; yet, with hard work, James had succeeded in solving the puzzle. He'd beaten Angus this round of the treasure-hunting game. He recited a clue aloud just for the pleasure of it: "'Christe Jesus told the story, yet He willna own the doubloon's glory, nor even a wee tithe of the treasure near.'"

Corny shook his head. "How did you memorize that stuff?"

"I've studied it enough."

"Strange clue, especially for your great-great-great-great-grandfather. Not exactly the religious type." Corny haw-hawed, his squinty blue eyes disappearing into rosy chapped cheeks. "Who woulda thought some dusty Sunday school story would help you find the right spot to dig?"

"Maybe the old pirate's father made him attend church when he was a boy." James reached into the pocket of his mackinaw and pulled out a copy of the map he'd sketched from the centuries-old original. "Now to find the treasure itself."

"Too bad Angus couldn't just mark the longitude and latitude where he hid the chest and be done with it." Corny shifted his brawny body to block the wind.

"Too smart for that." James had explained this before. "Corny, Angus *stole* from his captain, Sir Francis Drake. He had to fool Drake, his enemies, and probably his friends too. He couldn't make a map that would spell it out." He gripped the paper, flapping in the gale like an angry gull. "You game to explore Wild Woman Waters tonight?"

"What? Where those Indian caves are?" Corny's enthusiasm slipped another notch. "You think the treasure's *there?*"

"I do." James pointed to the bay on the map, a quarter mile away. "It fits the next clue:

'How canna forget the bonnie wench,
Witchy hair fallin' to her knee?
Strong lass a-dancin', soaper a-dancin',
Luve and gowld for me, but death to thee.'"

"At least he's not quotin' a Sunday School lesson in this one." Corny leaned on his shovel. "Can't we celebrate the coin tonight and explore the caves in daylight?"

"Too public, and you know it." James scoffed, "You'd let a few spooky Indian stories scare you away from the treasure?"

Something of his own flaming desire reignited that of his first mate. Corny stuck out his chin. "Ain't nothing going to keep me from finding that big ol' chest of gold."

"That's the spirit." James clapped the lad on the back. "With the draft on, we'd better find it fast ...."

James let his words die. Corny stared at the roiling waves. The Japanese attack on Pearl Harbor just before last Christmas had blown the world apart. Now war threatened their quest.

So far, Corny had escaped shipping out on the troop trains. In his twenties, James knew his own seafaring skills might eventually land him in combat at some point, but right now both men had been exempted from conscription because their work on James's cargo ship was considered "essential services." Corny and James also had joined the local volunteer flotilla of fishermen who, night and day, kept a lookout for Japanese submarine activity.

"Maybe they'll keep us here, patrolling the coastline," Corny said.

"That would make too much sense," James joked, trying to lighten the moment. "We'll probably find ourselves in foxholes a thousand miles from the nearest water."

Corny guffawed—he never worried too long about anything—shouldered his shovel, and followed James south.

As they fought the wind, James tried not to imagine searching for the treasure without Corny's endless energy and camaraderie. Yet, if Corny were drafted, who would listen to James's hopes and share the torrid joy of the treasure? James preferred not to kindle treasure lust in his more intelligent friends.

Still, his first mate's inevitable departure might work out for the best.

Lately, Corny had shown far too much interest in the Paisley treasure.

# 1

Apple Grove, Oregon, present day

"**D**rinks are on me, ladies!" Melanie Burkhart's yell, as she burst into Espresso Yourself, stunned the Purls of Hope knitting circle. She might as well have tossed firecrackers into their cozy corner.

Shannon McClain, owner of the coffeehouse and the Paisley Craft Market that housed it, handed her friend her usual caramel macchiato. "Sit and tell us the good news, or we won't get anything done tonight." She looked closer at Melanie. The dark-haired, forty-something woman's thin face, usually pale and composed, flushed candy pink. "Are you all right?"

Joyce Buchanan, a plump, bling-y blonde, threw aside the purple argyle sock she was knitting and trumpeted into an imaginary game show microphone: "She's won a ten-year supply of gen-u-ine color-coordinated French designer vacuum cleaner bags!" Joyce woo-hooed and offered Melanie a fake congratulatory hug. "Isn't this wonderful, folks? No wonder she's so excited!"

Melanie half-sputtered, half-giggled, unable to speak.

Shannon rolled her eyes at Joyce. As Melanie quieted, Shannon coaxed her, "Go on. Tell us."

"Tell us!" Betty Russo and Kate Ellis clamored.

"I'm still cancer free!" Behind Melanie's glasses, tears

pooled in her green-sparkle eyes. "The doctor said my chance of a recurrence has dropped significantly now."

"Are you serious, girl?"

"Group hug, group hug!"

The Purls leaped from their chairs and scrummed in a joyous dance.

Shannon embraced the happy tremor of Melanie's shoulders. *Cancer. Ugly word.* God willing, Melanie would never have to say it again.

"Why didn't you tell us you had an appointment in Portland?" Betty finally demanded in a half-happy, half-aggravated motherly tone. "One of us could have gone with you."

Kate wiped her eyes. "Did Greg take time off to go with you?"

"No, I didn't want to bother him. My son's been through enough." Melanie raised her chin. "You've all been through enough."

"As if you haven't." Shannon patted her shoulder. Not only had breast cancer ravaged her friend, but Melanie's no-good husband had left her the minute he'd learned her diagnosis. Shannon shot a warning look at Joyce, whose blue eyes held a wicked glint. *Don't say you're glad he's dead.*

"I'm so, so happy for you." Joyce waltzed Melanie around the room. Shannon breathed a sigh of relief. Maybe Joyce's past struggles with false accusations had taught her not to verbalize *everything.*

Shannon concocted another round of drinks, on the house. No way would she allow Melanie to pay for these. She wondered if life could get any better. Such incredible, loyal friends. While the Purls of Hope knit yarns into warm socks, hats, and throws for the needy, they also knit their lives into a friendship that never unraveled. Fiftyish Betty Russo, who owned The Apple Grove Inn with her husband, Tom, kept the Purls on track with her down-to-earth approach and a smile that brightened any situation. Kate Ellis, a dog lover, channeled kindheartedness into her business, Ultimutt Grooming, as well as into her friends. Melanie, a florist at the Flower Pot, said little but did much to support the other Purls. And dear, mouthy Joyce, the owner of Pink Sprinkles Bakery, gladly would have tossed her last coconut cream pie into the face of their enemy.

Though Shannon missed her twins, Lara and Alec, they enjoyed their classes at Portland State, and she was learning to channel her energies into her specialties: silversmithing and beadwork. Both her craft market and coffee shop had posted growing profits in the past year, and several prominent artists rented studios in her loft.

And, yes, her face grew warm when she thought of Hunter, who had come to Apple Grove to conduct marine research along the Oregon coast. Hunter, with his California surfer looks and sunlit smile, had brightened her world, reminding her how much she loved life.

Her phone rang. Lara? Hunter? She set the whipped cream on the granite counter and turned so the chattering Purls wouldn't see as she slipped her cell from her khakis pocket.

It was Deborah, her housekeeper. A ripple of disappointment disturbed the perfect flow of the moment.

*Hunter doesn't have to call every day,* Shannon admonished herself. *We haven't been dating that long.* She tapped the phone. "Deborah. What's up?"

No response.

"Hello?" Shannon checked the screen. Still connected?
"Oh, Shannon."

Fire alarms shrilled in her head. Her take-charge
employee and friend never sounded this agitated. "What's
wrong? Are you sick? Did the twins call?"

"No, no ... but ...."

"Tell me, dear." Shannon bit her lip. "Quick."

"Someone broke in."

"Broke in?" Shannon choked on the words. The Purls'
joyous henfest quieted, and they all stared at her as she
stuttered into her phone, "A-are you all right?"

"I'm OK. But I can't remember if I set the alarm before
I went shopping," Deborah wailed.

"Don't even think about it right now—"

A whisper-scream. "I think I hear the intruder—he's
still inside!"

"Lock yourself in the bathroom—"

"I did. I called 911."

"Try and stay calm. I'll be there in a minute." Shannon
hung up and flung off her apron.

So much for her perfect life.

\*     \*     \*

"Please don't go in there, Shannon." Deborah's voice
trembled. She clutched a large, outdated flashlight. For the
first time, Shannon's energetic white-haired housekeeper
looked old.

Trying to shrug off Deborah's concern, Shannon crept
toward the foyer's grand staircase. She raised the poker

she'd grabbed from the library fireplace. "The guy's probably gone, but if he's stupid enough to hang around, I'll make him wish he hadn't."

She slipped down a side hall to the back staircase. The door to the closet built under it stood wide open. Shannon inhaled whiffs of cedar as she ducked inside and pushed aside parkas that had fallen to the floor. She dodged skis and poles crisscrossed at crazy angles. The intruder had slid aside a panel in a sidewall of the closet, revealing a large hidden door that resembled a bank vault's entrance, complete with a large combination lock. It, too, stood open. Neither she nor Deborah—who had worked at the Paisley mansion for decades—had ever seen it before.

"I wonder what my grandparents kept in here?" Shannon whispered as she crept closer.

"Wait till the police come," Deborah pleaded.

*And let Chief Grayson wall me off from the crime scene in my own house?* She almost wished Deborah hadn't called 911. Shannon edged forward, sharp end of the poker pointed straight ahead.

She stopped just inside the vault's entrance. The cedar aroma gave way to an aged, papery smell, as if the tiny room had been sealed for years. For a moment, Shannon's lungs threatened to fold like fans, and she wanted to run from the close, cramped space. Instead, she focused on the dark cave before her. In the dim light, she detected no movement. No place to hide either. "He's gone, Deborah. Hand me the flashlight."

Shannon swept the secret room with the strong beam of light. Spider webs shrouded every corner. She scanned the dust-coated wooden floor with the beam again. Footprints!

Smooshed together as the burglar moved around, but clear enough to compare to her own feet. Much larger. Probably a man's.

*What was he after?*

Prickles of fear beaded her spine, but Shannon gave herself a pep talk. *These are like footprints in the snow. They'll help lead us to whoever did this.*

Shannon peered at shadowy rows of old books on shelves. Fuzzy miniatures of sailing ships gave the room a seaworthy feel. An antique compass and other navigational-looking instruments added to the effect. They probably could bring high prices. Why hadn't the thief taken them? Or had Deborah scared him off before he could steal them?

Shannon hated the thought of breathing the stale air, yet she longed to investigate. If she did proceed any farther, though, she might destroy evidence.

Would she even show the secret room to the police chief? She hadn't decided. Shannon pointed the flashlight at a small desk facing the wall, the only furniture in the small space. It had three drawers, one with a lock that looked as if someone had tampered with it. An empty kerosene lamp sat on top.

A chiming bell interrupted her inspection. *Blast.*

Shannon left the door open a tiny crack and slid the panel shut. While she pushed skis and poles against it, she called to Deborah, "Stall Grayson in the foyer!"

"Are you insane?" For a moment, Deborah sounded like herself. "Aren't you going to tell—"

"I'm not sure." Shannon hastily hung up coats.

The doorbell, pushy as the police chief himself could

be at times, demanded an answer. Shannon heard Deborah greet him. She played the frightened female with a quaver in her voice. Or maybe she wasn't acting? Shannon exited the closet and shut the door, scolding herself for ignoring her friend's trepidation. She brushed her clothes and hurried to the mansion's foyer.

Grayson, his thinning hair sticking up, was examining the front entrance keypad. She heard him mumble, "Perp must have been wearing gloves." Grayson hardly glanced at Shannon as he instructed one policeman to search inside. Officer Brownley nodded to her sympathetically before he and another officer split up to search the estate's yard and adjoining acreage. Grayson's right-hand man was a polite young fellow who didn't overstep his authority.

"Let's nail this down." Grayson's dark eyes bored into Deborah's red-rimmed ones. "The front door was standing open when you came home—unusual during a theft, but this house sits a long distance from the road, behind all these trees. Tell me, did you turn on the security system earlier, before you left the house?"

Shannon joined them. "May I fix Deborah a cup of tea? I'm sure she'll answer your questions with more clarity when she's recovered a bit."

Grayson bristled. As usual, he reminded Shannon of a temperamental bulldog. "First impressions are important. I want to get the facts down before she forgets them—"

"I'm not senile yet, thank you very much." A spark of Deborah's usual moxie flashed at him.

"But you may have forgotten to turn on the alarm?" Grayson asked.

Deborah wilted. "Yes."

"I forget occasionally too," Shannon said, wanting to reassure her housekeeper, who was wringing the hem of her sensible cardigan as if it were soaked.

Grayson's phone rang, and he growled into it. "Any sign of the perp?"

He barked more instructions, then turned back to them and said, "It looks like the guy rummaged through a couple of closets—one in the basement and one upstairs. No sign of him, though."

Shannon waited for him to say more. *Should that make us feel better?*

Grayson demanded, "If you forgot to turn on the alarm, how did the intruder know that?" He paused. "If you did turn on the alarm, how did he get past the security system?"

*How, indeed?* Michael Stone, a top-of-the-line security expert, had redesigned the system when a burglar had broken in soon after Shannon inherited the beautiful old house.

Grayson made valid points. She didn't like to think about the implications behind his words.

She also didn't like to think about Michael.

"I'm sorry, Chief Grayson." Deborah's quiet voice brought Shannon back to the present. Her housekeeper still clutched her sweater, but she lifted her chin. "I don't remember. I do know that I locked the door with my key. I hate all these gadgets and gizmos. From now on, though, I'll certainly pay more attention to them."

From the set of her mouth, Shannon knew Deborah meant what she said. *Look out, burglar. She may take a rolling pin to you next time.*

Grayson grunted. "Have you noticed anything missing?"

"Not yet," Shannon said truthfully. She didn't yet know if anything had been taken from the secret room.

"Check your belongings while I go over your security system, but touch stuff only if you have to. If you see anything odd, back off. Come and get me."

*Yes, sir!* Shannon wanted to salute him. Probably not a good idea.

She gestured to Deborah. "Would you check downstairs while I go up?"

The housekeeper's eyes darted toward the back closet. Shannon gave a miniscule shake of her head. *Don't tell him.*

Deborah blew out a nervous breath and headed for the dining room. Shannon hoped the intruder hadn't raided her Grandmother Victoria's silver, more for Deborah's sake than for her own. Shannon hadn't known her grandmother personally, so replacing it via insurance payment would not pain her deeply. She even let herself fantasize about designing new pieces. In Deborah's eyes, however, no new set, no matter how gorgeous, could replace the silver she had polished for decades while working for Victoria.

Going upstairs presented more of a challenge than Shannon anticipated. A thousand tiny hairs rose on her arms as she reached the top.

*Don't be a wimp.* The guy was gone. The officer said so. Shannon made herself check Lara's room, then Alec's. Lara's closet, stuffed with clothes, hadn't been touched, whereas Alec's sparse summer wardrobe and a few outgrown coats lay on his closet floor. Grayson had said the intruder had also searched a basement closet. Why do that, with plenty of expensive items in plain view?

Thank heaven, the kids had taken their electronics to college. Even if the guy had stolen Shannon's computer and external backup, she kept copies of everything in her store computer. Not much else upstairs a burglar would want, except the antique paintings on the hallway walls. He probably hadn't had time to grab those.

She hesitated outside her own door, not wanting to know if the creep had stolen her jewelry. Fortunately, she kept the exquisite locket that had triggered her American adventure in her bank's lockbox. But what about her pearls? She couldn't bear parting with the necklace her late husband, John, had fastened around her neck the Christmas before he died, or the tiny pearl earrings he'd given her as a bride. A familiar sweet ache brought back their wedding, with John so handsome in his clan's plaids ....

What if the burglar had made off with her rings? Her heartbeats thundered in her ears. After several years of widowhood, she'd only recently removed them from her hand.

Shannon bared her teeth at the thief. *You may have stolen my jewelry, but you can't steal my memories.*

She marched into her bedroom. Her white leather jewelry case sat on her dresser. She jiggled its clasp. Locked. She slipped the key from its hiding place in the closet and opened the case. The plain gold band and the ice-chip diamond in Shannon's engagement ring glimmered from their satiny cushions.

She leaned against the wall, limp with relief. Within seconds, though, she stiffened and ran to her nightstand. She yanked open the drawer.

"Yesss!" Her almost-completed bead project, a mosaic

hanging of Joseph wearing his coat of many colors, had not been sullied. Shannon hugged it to her chest, then unfolded it. She pressed the beads to her cheek, savoring their knobby comfort.

She wished she could hold the hanging forever, but she made herself place it back in her nightstand. Shannon searched the rest of the room, even checked under the massive canopy bed she'd inherited, though she couldn't think of a good reason why. Nothing missing.

"Shannon? Are you all right up there?" Deborah's voice floated up the stairs.

"I'm fine." Shannon scurried from the room and headed for the first floor. Deborah met her on the landing and wrapped her in a rare hug.

"So far as I can see, the guy took only those little marble Peruvian statues and the bronze vase from the foyer." Deborah's no-nonsense voice had returned. Her arms loosened their grip on Shannon, then dropped to her sides. "Not terribly bright of him, given all the valuable things your grandmother collected."

"Nothing's missing upstairs." Shannon smiled a little. "For that, we can be thankful."

They checked the basement together, then reported to Chief Grayson. He seemed almost annoyed that he'd devoted his afternoon to a thief who took so little. He sent his officers on other assignments via his phone, then asked Shannon, "Anybody know the security code besides you two?"

"My twins, of course."

He snorted. "College kids, right?"

"This is their home," Shannon snapped.

"And they have lots of friends, don't they? Friends who come here on weekends, stay here so they can go to the beach?" A note of sarcasm edged his voice. "Friends who may have gotten locked out at some point and begged for the code?"

Shannon ached to tell Grayson about the secret room, if for no other reason than to say, "This has nothing to do with my children or their friends. You're wrong, wrong, wrong."

But was he?